LADY OF THE NILE

VERONICA SCOTT

Cover Art by Fiona Jayde

To my daughters, Valerie and Elizabeth; my brother, David and my best friend, Daniel, for all their encouragement and support! And to Pauline B – hugs!

CHAPTER ONE

Facing down the attacking Hyksos hordes at the Meribe Pass had been easier in many ways than preparing to meet a grateful Pharaoh to receive the reward for not accepting defeat. Captain Khian walked the line of his small troop murmuring encouragement, straightening a sword here and making a joke there, anything to lighten the men's tension as they waited outside the ceremonial chamber for their moments under Pharaoh's eye. It wasn't often that common soldiers had the chance to stand in front of the Living God who ruled Egypt. The idea was terrifying.

At last the scribe touched his elbow. "You can march in now, captain."

He nodded, gave his soldiers one final, critical inspection. "We'll do the Jackal Nome proud, men."

Khian set the pace, walking behind the young scribe, keeping his proud military bearing, not looking to the right or the left but focusing on the glittering dais where Pharaoh's golden throne sat and the Great One himself waited to honor them. He might be only a landholder, commissioned to fight in the war against the invaders, rather than one of the career officers, and his men might be farmers in their daily lives, but by the gods, they'd held that damned pass and saved the day for Egypt. Pride for what his troops had accomplished in battle filled his heart and pushed aside trepidation over being in a completely foreign environment now. He just wanted to get through the ceremony without disgracing himself or his men in front of the ruler.

The scribe had them line up off to the side, awaiting their moment with Pharaoh, who was still speaking with a group of ambassadors. "Your name will be called and then move forward in front of the throne. Salute and stand at attention."

"We'll do as you instruct." Khian clenched his hand on the hilt of his sword. He gazed across the chamber while he waited, taking in the crowd of courtiers attending the audience. For the most part the nobles, officers and functionaries were a blur of painted faces, fine clothes and elaborate jewelry but one woman caught his attention. She sat near the queen, so was obviously high ranking, but her expression was sweet rather than haughty and she stared at him as if trying to give him encouragement. Could she tell he was nervous about committing an inadvertent error of royal protocol? The lady smiled, plying her ostrich feather fan flirtatiously. He made a slight bow to her, before he abruptly remembered where he was.

Ridiculous as it might seem, he felt as if he had a friend here.

Boredom had been weighing on Tuya all afternoon. She'd sat through many audiences at the court of Pharaoh Nat-re-Akhte and this one was no different— newly arrived dignitaries to greet, a few issues needing Pharaoh's judgment, gold of valor to be awarded to a deserving soldier or two. In her five years as chief lady-in-waiting to the Royal Wife, Tuya had seen all variations.

Pharaoh would present the gold of valor next, and Tuya found herself glancing at the assembled soldiers. The officer captured her attention instantly. Something about his face drew her gaze. He had the look of a man going into combat and she guessed his unfamiliarity with royal protocol and the customs at court might lie at the heart of his tension. Or he was worried for his men that they'd manage the moments under Pharaoh's scrutiny with honor. Direct attention from the living god was a frightening thing to most people. She wished she could take the officer aside for a moment and reassure him that Pharaoh was a kind man, a soldier himself in fact, and would most likely be tolerant of any minor breaches in protocol from overawed rural troops.

The captain was looking at the crowd now, as he waited, and when his attention turned to her, she smiled and tried to project encouraging thoughts for him. *It doesn't matter how the court perceives you, only Pharaoh's opinion counts with the gods.* She guessed something of her attitude might have come across, as he gave her a smile and a little bow. Tall and muscular, he really was handsome, with a strong jaw, chiseled cheekbones and piercing hazel eyes.

Of course, thinking of becoming better acquainted with the man was foolish. A high-ranking lady like her would never mingle with common soldiers from some remote province of Egypt. Her usual companions were the nobility and the highest ranking officers of the army.

"Captain Khian of the Jackal Nome," said the chief scribe, "And his personal honor guard, drawn from members of his provincial command, to represent the rest."

The officer stepped forward, his plain blue cloak swirling around his legs. Six soldiers stood ramrod straight behind him and all saluted.

Pharaoh leaned forward to speak to the solider. "My general tells me your men held off the enemy at the Meribe Pass long enough for him to bring up reinforcements and turn the tide of battle. Well done." He took the gold of valor, a heavy necklace of golden flies, from the scribe and looped it over the captain's neck.

"It was either dig in and fight or jump off the cliffs at our back, Great One." This Khian's voice was deep, his smile engaging. "I didn't see much choice in the moment, frankly. So we made a wall of our shields and dared the Hyksos to overrun us."

Tuya held her fan still, waiting to see how the ruler would react to being addressed. Normally, the recipients of honors merely saluted and murmured their brief, awed thanks.

But Pharaoh was a former military man and in a good mood. He laughed. "Sometimes the best strategy is just to survive and fight like hell, captain, I quite agree." He addressed the scribe at his side. "A land grant and a writ of amkhu for the captain."

Tuya was surprised. Amkhu, the honor of being buried at Pharaoh's expense, was rarely bestowed these days.

Pharaoh continued, "Extra commendation to all members of his company and a gold bar for each man."

Never at a loss, even when faced with unexpected requests, Edekh, chief scribe of all Egypt, turned to his assistant scribe, who handed him two scrolls. A tiny table was brought, the scrolls unrolled and held in place by servants, as Pharaoh impressed his seal into melted red wax.

"With Egypt's gratitude." Pharaoh handed the scrolls to the officer personally.

Tuya shook her head in wonder. This man and his soldiers must have accomplished quite a feat, no matter how low-key the discussion today was. Receiving the scrolls from the hand of the Great One was an incredible distinction.

Captain Khian saluted, his men following suit, and withdrew from the chamber, led by a scribe who stepped to his elbow when it was clear Pharaoh had completed what he wished to say. The group marched past Tuya, and she was surprised when Khian glanced sideways in her direction, inclining his head again ever so slightly.

She flickered her fan in front of her face as she blushed. The lady next to her leaned over, giggling. "Was the rustic flirting with you? Here, in front of the entire court?"

"Did the queen see?"

"No, calm yourself, Tuya, no one saw but me. Don't worry; there'll be no vicious gossip about you today, nor merciless teasing about your new taste for commoners. Your momentary inattention went unnoticed." Her friend laughed and switched her focus to the next group claiming Pharaoh's attention and the audience continued.

The next day she wasn't on the roster of ladies-in-waiting, but she was required to perform her duties at the temple of Mut, as one of many part-time priestesses participating in a ritual for the blessing of the changing season. She danced and sang and chanted as required, having performed the ceremony hundreds of times since being taught the requirements as a child. Not meaning any disrespect to the goddess, nevertheless today she found her mind wandering more than once, despite the pageantry around her.

When the ceremony was done, most of the noble ladies like herself strolled to their litters, anxious to return to their homes, or to the palace. It was late afternoon by that time, and Tuya split off from the group to walk toward her favorite spot on the temple grounds—the small garden with the reflecting pool, tucked away in a far corner. She thought of it as her secret—hers and the goddess's, since a large statue of Mut with her wings outstretched was perched on a pedestal across from the pond.

As usual, the place was deserted, save for the turtles sunning themselves on the pond's broad stone rim. Tuya sat on the bench, leaning against the sun warmed wall and exhaled heavily, closing her eyes. *Another day nearly done, just like the one before and the hundreds before that. And the million to come before I see my tomb, no doubt.* Opening her eyes and sitting upright as a lady of the court should, she spoke to the goddess. "What's ever going to change?"

There was no answer from Mut.

Bothered by her nagging sense of discontent, Tuya heaved a sigh and slumped again. It was good Egypt knew peace and prosperity; the Nile flowed and flooded as it should, and Pharaoh sat a secure throne. She loved Ashayet the Royal Wife and relished the honor of being a lady-in-waiting. She was equally proud of her service to the goddess in whose garden she sat. "But is there nothing else?"

Shutting her eyes, she was annoyed to feel unshed tears. No less than three ladies-in-waiting had left the court this year with the queen's blessing, going to be married and raise families. Several priestesses had done the same. It seemed to Tuya advantageous possibilities and adventure had passed her by somehow when she wasn't paying attention, and now she was locked into this life of service to others, never to have one of her own.

Soothed by the afternoon's warmth, she allowed her eyelids to drift downwards for a moment. No rush to get back to the palace.

She stood on a hill, in the shade of a beautiful palm tree, watching groups of people walk along a path across the river from her. They danced and laughed and kissed and talked amongst themselves, as if going to a wonderful festival or special event. Men and women strolled hand in hand, oblivious to anything but each other. Families traveled in little groups, the babies in adult arms, toddlers and young children skipping and running ahead, only to rejoin their parents.

"How do I get over there?" Shielding her eyes with her hand, she searched for a path leading away from where she stood, or a bridge to cross the river.

"But you positioned yourself here, why do you now want to leave?"

Surprised, Tuya turned to the woman standing beside her whose presence she hadn't noticed before, being so intent on the parade across the way. She seemed familiar, but no name came to Tuya's tongue. "I didn't choose to stand here."

"Indeed you did. You worked hard and cleverly to achieve this elevated role. Don't you remember all the times you chose the path of service over more demanding—and perhaps frightening—opportunities? Opted for the safety of the familiar?"

"I never—"

"You refused numerous offers for your hand, stating you couldn't leave Ashayet early in her term as Royal Wife, or when she was pregnant or nursing or later as a young mother."

"I was needed!"

"The Royal Wife has fifty ladies-in-waiting, with dozens more who'd relish the chance for the appointment for a year or two."

"I also serve the goddess at the temple."

The woman laughed. "As one of a hundred. Did anyone other than the goddess notice when you stopped singing today? Or started again?"

Feeling a chill, and a bit frightened at her unknown companion's knowledge, Tuya searched again for a path to the river. A low wall surrounded the spot where she stood, and she got goosebumps when she realized there was no break, no exit. She could step over the rows of nearly laid bricks but fear made her pause.

"Where are they all going?" she asked.

"They travel the road of life," the woman said. "With all the experiences, good and bad, you've chosen to shield yourself from. The highs and the lows of a life *lived*. Not merely observed, not simply drifted through, like a ship caught in the backwaters of the Nile. *You* chart a safe course going nowhere except the tomb."

A sudden fear entered Tuya's mind like a slithering cobra. "Am I going to be in trouble when my heart is judged?"

"No, for you've committed no crimes against the gods or Egypt, told no lies." The woman tapped her on the chest. "Your heart is true but untried, untouched. Indeed, many envy you for your closeness to Pharaoh and his Royal Wife, for your comfortable, easy life in the palace." The other shook her head, causing the gold and turquoise beads in her hair to chime. "You represent potential untapped. A waste, but nothing to punish." She gathered her fine linen skirts in one hand, preparing to leave the enclosure.

Greatly daring, for Tuya now realized she was in a vision and the person with her was either a goddess or a servant of the Great Ones, she put her hand on the lady's arm to detain her. "Is there time to change?"

Laughing, the woman shifted away from her. "You? Change your path now?" She gestured at the wall surrounding them. "You're close to the point where destiny is completely set. Shai the god of Fate only has so much patience, waiting to see what a human will do with their choices, and you've exhausted his. He's moved on to others."

Terrified, Tuya realized while they'd been chatting, more rows of bricks had been laid by invisible hands and the barrier was higher. "I don't serve Fate, I serve Mut."

Shaking a beringed finger at her, the other said, "All but the Great Ones are subject to Fate. Rare indeed is the intervention by a god or goddess on a human's behalf."

"Why show me all this then?" Tuya stared at the procession of people across the river, still happily moving through what she now understood were their lives. As she watched, several solitary men and women greeted each other and continued their walk hand in hand. Her heart ached as she recalled several good, worthy men she'd had as lovers but who drifted away when she refused to commit to marriage. It'd been a long time since she'd even exerted herself to flirt and seek a new lover. She couldn't remember the last time a nobleman or high ranking officer had sought her out.

"Perhaps the goddess has a soft spot for you. Perhaps she had hopes for one who was a favorite."

The breeze lifted the curls of Tuya's elaborate wig and brought the scent of the blue lotus to her nostrils. "Change is terrifying to me, ever since I was a child and my father died. Our whole world shattered and nothing was ever the same again." She wrapped her arms around herself, seeking to keep the grief and frightening memories of the years after his death at bay. "How can I risk suffering such upheaval again? How can anyone blame me for creating a life of safe comfort?"

Patting her arm, the other said, "Only you can decide if you wish to break the wall of the sheltered life you've created. Don't wait too long."

And she turned into a bird and was gone, winging toward the river on ivory white wings.

Tuya's back hurt. Opening her eyes, she stretched, amazed to find herself reclining on the hard stone bench in Mut's tiny garden. *I fell asleep?* More than a little afraid, she craned her neck to look at the statue of the goddess, but the carving was unchanged, Mut's face serene as always. Tuya realized the light was going fast as Ra's sun boat glided over the western bank of the Nile.

Unable to believe how long she'd been napping, or more correctly, caught in the goddess-sent vision, she got to her feet with difficulty, stiff after lying on the unforgiving bench, and hastened down the path toward the area where the litters waited. Stumbling a bit, she was relieved to see her conveyance and servants, although dismayed to find hers was the only one left.

"My lady, thank the gods, you're here." Hemaka, the chief of her household, straightened from where he'd been leaning against the gilded litter.

"Why didn't you come check on me?" she asked. "We're late."

"It's not my place to interrupt your devotions," he said, eyebrows raised. "You've made the rule clear in the past." He helped her into the litter and, as she settled against the cushions, he gestured for the four men to raise the elongated chair into the air and start marching. "We'll have to return to the palace through the city, my lady."

"Is using city streets a good idea, so late in the day? Why can't we take the private road, as we usually do?"

"No one uses it after dark," he reminded her. "There will be no guards and it's possible thieves will be keeping an eye out for anyone unwary enough to risk the route."

She toyed with her ornate golden collar. "But at this hour, with the work day complete, the people of the city will be in the roads and the squares—it'll be crowded."

"The situation can't be helped." He leaned over. "Best you pull your cloak closed, conceal the richness of your attire."

As she complied, she thought with regret of the palace guards to which she was entitled by virtue of being senior among Ashayet's ladies. She hadn't requested an escort today because she was with other noblewomen priestesses, and there'd been an honor guard for the entire complement from the palace. Tuya was angry with herself for being careless about the time of day. *But if the goddess wished to send me a vision, there wasn't anything I could do about it.* She shied away from contemplating the substance of the vision, even though every moment was clear in her mind.

Moving quickly, the litter bearers entered the edge of the main square. Keeping the pace, Hemaka directed them to work their way along the fringe and Tuya relaxed a bit as she hoped she might reach the palace with no problem after all. Even as she had the thought, shouts sounded up ahead and the litter slowed.

"Two men, arguing," Hemaka said, tall enough to see over the heads of those surrounding them. "And a crowd gathering to watch, making bets."

Forward progress became impossible. Tense, Tuya sat upright on the litter and stared at her servants in the flickering torchlight. "What do we do? Should someone run to the palace for help?"

"Well, what do we have here?" The voice was harsh, the accent thick. "Are you lost, pretty lady?"

There were jeering laughs from the companions of the man who'd spoken. Reinforced by their approval, he swaggered closer, thumbs hooked in his belt.

Tuya forced herself to take a deep breath. "I'm returning to the palace. Kindly move out of my way."

"We'd escort you. For a price." The heavyset man came closer, shoving a protesting Hemaka out of his way with ease. "Or we might escort you somewhere else. Someplace private." He gestured at his comrades, who pressed closer. "We're guests in your fair city – shouldn't you be more welcoming?"

She smelled stale beer on his breath and shrank back when he reached for her. "How dare you threaten to lay hands on me? I'm a member of the Pharaoh's court."

"Pharaoh should take better care of his ladies then." The thug grabbed her by the arm and tried to drag her from the cushions.

A thug tripped the litter bearer on the front left corner and the platform tilted, spilling her to the ground. She landed hard on her side, breaking her fall awkwardly, biting her lip from the pain.

There were shouts and the sounds of men running and the next thing she knew, a man had placed himself between her assailant and Tuya. Sword raised, he said, "Show proper respect to your betters or the edge of my blade will sever that unruly tongue from your head."

"Apologies." The man bowed his head but eyed the soldier slyly. "You don't have enough men with you to arrest all of us. I've my entire crew here with me."

"I'm concerned with getting the lady to the palace, where she belongs, and nothing else. If you leave now, I'll forget your face. Go seek trouble elsewhere while I'm busy here."

Laughing, the street tough pivoted and strutted away.

Sheathing his sword, her rescuer bent over to lift Tuya to her feet. "Drunken sailors from Minos. Scum. Are you all right, my lady?"

"My—my wrist hurts." Dazed from the fall, she stared at him in the flickering torchlight. "You seem familiar. Thank you for your timely assistance."

He kept his gentle hold on her as he checked how efficiently his squad of men had routed the other bystanders and would-be trouble makers. Then he gave his full attention to her. "Captain Khian, at your service, my lady. If I may be so bold, we saw each other at Pharaoh's audience a few days ago."

She put a hand to her head to straighten her wig. "Oh yes, I remember now. Congratulations on your gold of valor."

"Kind of you to remember. As I told the Great One, we merely stood our ground and fought." Khian checked her wrists, first one then the other, sliding his strong fingers across her skin with a reassuring touch. "Nothing broken. A sprain perhaps, when you attempted to break your fall." He took a scarf from her belt, ignoring her exclamation of protest and made a rapid sling, looping it over her neck and supporting the affected wrist. "How does that feel?"

Realizing his intent had only been to help, she smiled. "Much better, thank you. How is it you're here, captain? I'm grateful, of course—"

Her servants had righted the litter, and Khian handed her into it, making sure the pillows were adjusted behind her back. "Move out," he said to Hemaka. "We'll accompany you to the palace, my lady, make sure there are no more unfortunate incidents."

His small squad took positions flanking her litter bearers and they proceeded, the soldiers clearing a path with their shields, knocking aside any drunken reveler who didn't move out of the way fast enough.

Khian remained by her side, keeping up easily with her litter even as he chatted. "We have three months left to serve, so Pharaoh was gracious enough to assign us to duty here in the city rather than returning to the front lines, where we might be held past our scheduled release date." He shot her a glance. "I have planting to oversee at home. The growing seasons don't wait for the concerns of men."

"No, I suppose not." Tuya knew her voice sounded dubious. She'd never given any energy to contemplating farming.

"Tonight my men and I are augmenting the regular troops who keep order in the city. Apparently, an argument broke out between rival factions of a builder's guild and then, of course, other predators circle while the patrols are kept busy. As you experienced."

Her head was swimming and the pain in her wrist was partially alleviated by support from the sling. She focused on his deep voice, so reassuring. "How did you know I was in trouble?"

"I observed movement in the crowd, as some new event drew their attention, like hyenas. You shouldn't be out so late unaccompanied."

"I stayed overlong at the temple." She bit her tongue. She didn't owe this man an explanation—it was his duty to come to her aid, no matter what her reasons might have been for the lateness of her journey home. But unaccountably she didn't want him to think less of her.

"Nearly at the palace, my lady," Hemaka said.

"I'll see you to the gates, then I must return to my duty station," Khian said.

When they arrived at Pharaoh's palace, the captain of the guard himself came to greet Tuya, red cloak swirling. The glittering gold accents, stiffly pleated linen kilt and sleek leather trim of his uniform was a stark contract to Khian's more humble blue cape, simple kilt and plain blue head cloth.

"She needs the care of a physician," Khian said, saluting with a fist to his heart. "Her wrist—"

"She'll be seen to," the other officer replied impatiently. "Her welfare now is hardly your concern. Lady Tuya, why didn't you have a proper detachment of guards?"

"I was foolish and stayed too long at the temple. Captain Khian and his men were kind enough to rescue me from difficulties in the great square." The tone the officer used to Khian displeased her, even if the higher ranking man was one of Pharaoh's Own, the elite cadre.

As Hemaka and the soldier helped her from the litter and started up the stairs, she forced them to pause for a moment. Looking over her shoulder, pleased to see Khian watching her, she said, "Thank you for your help, captain. I can't add to the gold of valor Pharaoh heaped upon you, but please accept my gratitude."

"It was my honor." He bowed, flashing a smile, then formed his men into two lines and marched away without another word or backward glance.

"You can send a special ration to his barracks," the officer said to her as they continued up the stairs. "If you really feel the need to recognize his help."

CHAPTER TWO

She had to endure a mild scolding from the Royal Wife for not being sensible about her return time from the palace, and a few days of discomfort while her sprained wrist healed, but Tuya found her life settled into its normal routine as easily as the waters of the Nile closed over a rock dropped into its flow. She puzzled over the vision she believed she'd had, but even if she wanted to change aspects of her life, where did one begin? And how could she give up her much envied position as one of Ashayet's companions? What would she do, if she didn't have a place at court?

Seated in the small private garden attached to her chambers in the palace, she was contemplating these questions yet again and fighting a headache when Hemaka knocked at the door.

"Pardon me for disturbing you, my lady, but you've received a message."

Heart beating faster for a moment, she thought of the handsome rural captain. *Maybe he wonders how I'm faring.* She held out her hand. "The scroll?"

Hemaka shook his head. "Nothing so formal. Your old nurse sent one of her grandsons this afternoon while you were playing senet with the Royal Wife. I was summoned to the far gate to meet with him."

Disappointed and feeling a bit foolish, she leaned back in her chair. "How is Behenu? Well, I hope."

Hemaka leaned close and lowered his voice. "She wishes to see you tonight at her home behind her son's inn, on a most urgent matter. You're to come alone and bring something of value."

Tuya covered her eyes with one hand and clenched her other on the chair arm. "You and I both know what those words mean. He promised to stay clear of Thebes after the last time."

"Will you go?"

With a deep sigh, she sat up. "Of course—I can't refuse my brother. Can you get me a plain dress and cloak from one of the maids?" Suddenly panicked, she grabbed his arm. "You will go with me tonight, won't you? I can't very well ask Pharaoh for a guard escort since my brother's under an order of exile."

"Need you ask?" The elderly servant seemed offended as he straightened his spine, but he patted her hand. "Of course, for all the good I can do if we're accosted, like the other night in the square."

Tuya shuddered. She'd had nightmares about the unpleasant events.

Speaking with the freedom of a servant who'd known her since childhood, he scowled. "It's long past time he stops looking to you for help with his problems. You've bailed his leaky boat for him too often."

Surprised by his tone, she said, "But he's my brother and he means well—"

"Half-brother." His acid tone didn't surprise her. Hemaka was an old family retainer from her late father's family and had never thought highly of her mother's second marriage or the child she'd given her new husband. "He keeps getting into unsavory situations. As he's grown older, the messes have gotten worse. Have a care, my lady. You don't want to jeopardize your own place at court. Pharaoh is well disposed to you, but even a Great One has limits to his generosity."

"Anen was caught in a problem not of his own making. He was innocent—"

Hemaka shook his head. "Too often you see only the small child who dogged your steps as a baby. He's a man grown, and one who makes poor choices." Mouth set in a thin line, the elderly servant spoke with the confidence of one who knows himself immune from reproach. From past arguments with him Tuya was well aware nothing she could say to Hemaka would make him see any good in Anen. Hemaka cared only about her well-being but his truculent attitude toward Anen sometimes made her defend her half-brother all the more. She couldn't seem to stop herself.

She walked to her jewelry box and flipped open the gaily painted lid, trying to decide which of her favorite rings she could part with now to help Anen. She'd given him so many things already over the last few years. "But no matter the past, how can I refuse to go see him and at least hear his news? Maybe there is no problem this time, maybe he stopped in Thebes to see me."

Hemaka raised his eyebrows but argued no further.

Long after the evening meal, she slipped out of a side gate of the palace, dressed in a plain gown and wrapped in a brown cloak obscuring her features. Tuya wore no jewelry, although she had three fine golden rings in a pouch tied to her belt. Hemaka stayed close by her side, leaning on a stout cane he could wield as a weapon if the occasion arose. The guards made no comment as she left the sanctuary of the palace grounds. She hoped gaining entry when she returned would be as simple. Spending the night at her nurse's small set of rooms behind a rowdy inn wasn't an appealing idea.

Tuya and Hemaka made good time through the city toward the waterfront area where the woman's sons had established their inn. There'd been a major parade earlier in the day, and the mood of the city was festive, as Pharaoh had provided the customary free bread and beer for all. Tuya encountered no difficulties on this trip and few spared even a second glance for a peasant woman with her elderly companion. They'd nearly reached their destination when Captain Khian, in a plain kilt and tunic, not his uniform, barred their way.

"It *is* you," he said. "What are you doing in this area at this time of night, in such a guise?"

Tuya knew it would be useless to argue, since he obviously recognized her, even in the uncertain light of the torches set along the road. Stranding tall, she tried to brazen it out. "None of your business, so if you'll permit me to be on my way." She tried to sidestep him, but he neatly blocked her, taking her firmly by the arm and pulling her aside. Glancing nervously at the rough area of the city they were traversing, Hemaka trailed behind.

"This costume is better suited to the time and place than what you wore the other night, but you don't belong here. Why are you taking such a risk?"

"I—I have to meet someone and you'll make me late."

He made a dismissive sound and maintained his grip. "A lover? In the depths of the Theban slums? Try again, for I'll not believe that tale of a court lady."

"My lady, the appointed hour is close," Hemaka said behind them.

Khian frowned at her. "Plainly an urgent matter to lure you from the palace at night and dressed like this."

"Not a lover," she said. "My—my old nurse is ill, and I need to see to her care." She didn't dare admit the presence of her brother, a criminal in exile, not even to a provincial officer temporarily stationed in Thebes. Word of Anen's trip to Thebes couldn't get out.

"Swear to me this entire affair is no risk to Egypt and Pharaoh."

Astonished, she stared at him open mouthed. "Of course not. I'd never do anything disloyal to the Black Lands or my ruler." Technically, of course, her brother was under an order of banishment after falling in with the wrong crowd. And being implicated in a plot to defraud Pharaoh of lawful taxes...but her brother had only come to see her, his sister, tonight. He was reformed, an honest—if unlucky—trader. Still, her conscience pricked her. She hoped this deception wasn't enough to cause her a problem when her heart was weighed for Judging after her death.

"I ought to mind my own business and leave you to your own devices since you're so bent on trouble, but my mother didn't raise me to leave a woman in a precarious situation. I'll accompany you."

Tuya stared at him. "You can't."

"Then we remain here." He leaned closer, softening his voice. "As we both saw the other night, Thebes after dark isn't a safe place for a woman to travel, especially with only one servant. I'm sworn to serve Pharaoh and his court, which puts you into the basket of those I should watch over. And I've been assigned to patrol these less-than-desirable areas of the city. You might be grateful for my sword."

"You're off duty," she said, gesturing at his attire. "And my errand is none of your business."

"You're right and I apologize for interfering. I shouldn't have asked the nature of your excursion. But please let me see to your safety. I can't walk away in good conscience."

"Oh, let him come," Hemaka begged. "We attract too much attention."

The idea of a sturdy soldier at her back, especially since her destination was a down-on-its luck inn, was appealing. She ducked around Khian and continued her progress toward the inn. "Come then, but be prepared for boredom."

The inn of the Leaping Perch was no better and no worse than any other establishment at the edge of the river district. Tuya didn't enter the inn itself but went to the rear, to where her nurse had a large house for herself and her family, making her home on the second floor, where she caught the cooling breezes at sunset and dawn. Gathering her skirts, Tuya prepared to climb the exterior stairs. "I don't suppose you'll wait here?"

Khian shook his head. "I'd rather not, my lady. What if some problem arises? I'd be too far away to be of any help to you." He watched her for a moment. "I swear on my honor as a soldier to stand guard only. Your business is not mine to know, as you made clear. If this evening's jaunt doesn't touch on Pharaoh's concerns, I've no official right to ask for more details. Only the concern of a would-be friend."

Worried he'd attract too much attention lingering, she conceded. "All right, follow me then."

Hemaka scrambled up the risers in front of her, complaining under his breath about his aged knees, which Tuya silently acknowledged with a pang of guilt was true enough. He would suffer in the morning for the unaccustomed exertion. She followed, with the stubborn captain on her heels. By the time she pushed aside the woven mat covering the doorway, there was no sign of her brother in the large common room.

Her nurse rushed forward to hug her. "You look more beautiful each time I see you, my lotus petal," she said. "Which isn't often enough."

"We can go to your bedroom to talk in private," Tuya said, assuming her brother had ducked in there to avoid being seen by Khian. "My friend can wait here until it's time for him to escort me back to the palace. Have you any beer?"

"None for me," Khian said immediately. "Go ahead, ladies. Hemaka will keep me company."

The comradely proximity of the two men was what Tuya feared, knowing her aged servant disapproved of this excursion, but she followed the nurse into the bedroom. Finger to her lips, Behenu led her across the room and out onto a balcony at the rear, where a ladder gave access to the roof. Leaning close and obviously enjoying the intrigue, the elderly woman whispered, "Your brother is waiting for you up there."

With a muttered curse, for she disliked heights, Tuya kilted her skirt and climbed the rickety ladder. Her brother was indeed pacing back and forth, but he helped her up the last few rungs onto the roof. He gave her a perfunctory hug as she got her balance then moved away to sit on the pile of cushions under the awning in the corner.

"Who's the man?" her brother asked, annoyance making his voice snap like a whip. "I said to come alone."

"Keep your voice down." She moved to join him, already working to undo the knot holding the small sack to her belt. "He's no one, a nosy army officer who appointed himself my guard when he accidentally met me out this late at night." Opening the cloth bag, she extracted the three rings, with a small pang of regret, because one was a favorite of hers, a gift from the Royal Wife, set with coral in the shape of a cat, and offered them to Anen.

In the moonlight she saw his frown. "That's all? These will hardly pay for my caravan passage to…well to where I'm going next. On business, mind you."

"They were all I could get my hands on with such short notice. I don't have stacks of deben at my disposal, you know. Living in the palace as I do, all my needs are taken care of by the Chief Scribe's administrators. If you don't want them—"

The rings disappeared into a pocket in his robe. "Better than nothing. Sorry if I sounded abrupt, sister dear. Being here in Thebes makes me nervous."

"Why are you here?"

"To see you, of course." Anen pulled her off balance for a kiss on the cheek. "I couldn't be this close to my beloved sister and not make the effort. To hell with the risk. It's been too long since we had a chance to talk." He gestured at the low table beside the cushions. "Behenu gave me dinner, not the best I ever ate, but filling. There are dates left, if you're hungry."

"I'm fine." She settled more comfortably into the pillows. He towered over her, having taken after his father, and was thin but wiry in build. "You look well—do I see a new tattoo?"

Anen glanced at his wrist in the torchlight. "Just something I took a fancy to. You like it?"

"I've never seen a butterfly and a scorpion together before." She studied the ink marked on his skin and found the design vaguely repulsive. Tuya tried for tact. "Seems like an odd combination of creatures—what does it mean?"

"It's kind of a secret group I belong to." Seeing her expression, he rushed on with the explanation. "Nothing ominous, beloved sister, I swear. We're a group of adventurers, merchants sworn to uh help each other with special deals, without others knowing of the association."

She was happy to change the subject to a topic other than the tattoo and who he might be associating with. "How is the trading business going? Did you make the deal you wanted on the ivory and furs?"

"Ivory and—oh yes, indeed I did. Turned a pretty profit. But then my ship sank in the strait, taking all my cargo straight to the bottom. I barely escaped with my life. 'Tis a wondrous tale." He gave her a smattering of details, which sounded familiar, but she decided she must be tired for surely he'd never written her of this shipwreck nor sent her word.

Anen always had a hard luck tale, though. On occasion the irreverent belief that Shai the god of Fate took a personal interest in ruining her brother's earnest attempts to better himself crossed her mind.

Her brother shook his head. "But enough of my troubles. How are you, sister dear? Any prospects for a husband as yet? The overeager captain downstairs, perhaps?"

She blushed, pleased he was taking an interest in her. "No, no one. Certainly not him—he's from a rural province and only here for a short time. I sometimes think I've become a piece of the palace furniture in the eyes of the court, everyone is so accustomed to my presence."

"So you stick to your routine?"

"Nothing changes." Idly, she picked a date and nibbled at it.

"Come with me," he said, spreading his arms and grinning. "See the world, have an adventure."

Startled, Tuya dropped the date onto the floor. "Are you mad? I can't do that."

"Why not? You've served the queen long enough, longer than most. She won't mind if you go off to live your own life now. I'll deck you in fine dresses and sparkling jewels, and we'll find you a husband. I know many a virile sea captain or wealthy caravan owner who'd be happy to woo a noblewoman, even one a bit past the usual age of marriage."

She ignored the backhanded compliment and searched by the uncertain lamplight for the dropped fruit to buy herself time. Could this be the answer to what the goddess had told her about changing her life? What Anen proposed was more than mere change but rather the total uprooting of her existence.

For a moment it was oddly tempting to contemplate doing something so out of character and surprising everyone, proving them wrong about her. But then reality crashed in. Anen could barely support himself—hadn't he taken three of her finest rings tonight and said even that wasn't enough? What kind of life would they live? Placing the date on the edge of the table, she said, "It's kind of you to want to make my life more exciting, but I fear I'd be a hindrance to you. I—I'm too used to being settled in one place, and safe."

"Danger's the spice for this boring existence," he said. "There's nothing better than risking all you possess, life included, on a toss of the gaming sticks, and no more exhilarating rush than the triumph of winning in the teeth of the jackals."

Tuya stared at him, unable to think of an adequate response.

With a yawn, stretching his arms wide, Anen rose. "I'd better be going. Can't be lingering in the city openly at dawn, when the first patrols make their rounds." He held out his arms. "Give your brother a hug?"

They embraced for a moment then Anen stepped to the far edge of the roof, making the short jump to the next roof. He gave her a wave and proceeded to climb down the ladder on the side of the other building.

She watched him go, worn out as always by time spent in his presence. He was charming and suave, and full of plans like this mad idea she should go with him. Sighing, Tuya crossed to the ladder and made her way to the nurse's bedroom.

Khian caught her in his strong arms and lifted her inside. "I was coming to check on how much longer we might be in returning to the palace. It'll be dawn soon. Imagine my surprise to find your nurse snoring in her bed and no sign of you, my lady." He led her quietly to the outer chamber, although Tuya knew nothing but thunder from the god Set would awaken her nurse once she'd fallen asleep.

"Is your business successfully concluded?" he asked.

"Not that it's any of your concern, but yes. I'm going to the palace now, if you wish to continue this annoying behavior."

"I gave my word to keep you safe this night."

They descended the stairs to the first floor, woke the dozing Hemaka, and let themselves into the street. Tuya was tired and worried how she'd maintain her duties today at Court, after a night spent walking from one end of Thebes to the other and catching up on her brother's news and adventures.

"I wish I could have hired you a chair," Khian said, "But even if I found any at this late hour, a servant such as your disguise proclaims you to be wouldn't be able to afford such a luxury."

"Thank you for the considerate impulse," she said, touched at his concern despite his obvious irritation with her. "I'll make it."

She was exhausted, her legs trembling by the time they reached the palace gate.

"Let me talk to the guard," Khian said. "Wait here."

She leaned on the wall and fought not to doze off. The first rays of the sun heralding Ra in his mighty boat sailing the skies appeared as Khian walked back to her. "Go quickly," he said. "The guard will look the other way, believing you a maid I've spent the evening with."

"My reputation—"

He pulled her hood up so it shadowed her face. "You risked your good name and more when you chose to sneak out to meet whoever the mysterious man was." He took her elbow and towed her to the gate. "Hurry, the guard changes in a few moments, and I don't know the men on the next shift. If you want to get safely inside without a long explanation of your true identity and why you were in the city, we need to be quick."

At the gate he took her in his arms and kissed her soundly on the lips before pushing her across the threshold, Hemaka stumbling after. The old man forced her to keep walking when she would have stopped to give the rural captain a piece of her mind. She had to admit his embrace, rushed though it had been, was pleasant, his kiss warm and skillful. Khian had the powerful arms of an archer and the muscles of a hardened warrior.

"He had to make your parting look good for the guard," Hemaka said in a low voice. "The soldiers were staring."

She swallowed her anger and let him escort her to her suite of rooms. There was no time for anything but a quick bath, refreshing her makeup, and a change of clothes before she was on duty to accompany the Royal Wife at the morning meal.

Ashayet commented on how pale she was under her elaborate makeup. "I do hope you're not sickening. We have a special guest arriving today, an old battle comrade of my husband's, who in fact saved his life at great personal cost," she said. "Tadenhut brings his bride, who isn't accustomed to our formal ways. I'd hoped to assign you to shepherd her through court activities and rituals during her stay." The queen studied her face for a moment. "But if you're ill, I have many ladies who can step in."

Although the queen meant well, the impact of her remark hit Tuya like a dagger. Yet another reminder she was valued, but only one of many, easily replaced. "I'm merely tired, Great One, although I thank you for your solicitude. I had troublesome dreams and didn't sleep well."

"Oh? The lady who arrives today is a fortune teller, or so I'm told, with close ties to the god Shai himself. Perhaps she can divine the meaning of your dreams for you." Ashayet smiled broadly, pleased with providing a solution so promptly.

"I'll consult with her." *When the seven hells are flooded by the Nile.* The last thing Tuya felt she needed now was any more advice or any more discouraging news about her fate.

The couple arrived in mid-afternoon and were greeted by Pharaoh and the Royal Wife personally, with members of their court in attendance, including Tuya. She was surprised at the tremendous honor being done to this former soldier, but apparently his sacrifice to save Pharaoh in battle had been extraordinary. The nobleman's leg was twisted and withered from injuries, although strengthened by a cunningly designed wooden brace enabling him to walk with a cane. Mehyta, the wife, was a sweet and shy woman of common birth, and Tuya soon understood why the queen insisted she needed a designated companion. The woman seemed overwhelmed by the chattering ladies-in-waiting and the grandeur of Ashayet's chambers when they all retired to the queen's rooms.

Tuya and Mehyta sat in a corner of the vast audience room while the queen and her attendants played noisy, lively games of senet and jackals and hounds, gossiping all the while. Tuya exhausted all her standard topics of conversation and both women fell silent.

"You don't need to work so hard to entertain me," the noble's wife said. "Although it's kind of you. I enjoy observing people and storing up my impressions and memories to discuss with my husband later."

Feeling mildly jealous of anyone who had such a spouse to confide in when she had only herself, Tuya nodded. "As you wish. The queen has several special events arranged over the next few days for diversion, including a cruise on the Nile and a special performance of *The Shipwrecked Sailor*—" She stopped in midsentence, realizing with chagrin her brother had beguiled her with parts of the well-known play's events, claiming them for his own. *No wonder I thought I'd heard the details before.* She told herself he'd wished to entertain her, or possibly even tease her with a silly joke she'd failed to catch, but the fact was she was left unsettled by his deception.

"There is a task I wish very much to do while I'm here," Mehyta was saying.

Recalling her assignment to smooth the way for the rural lady, Tuya said, "I'm sure we can arrange whatever you desire."

"I'd like to visit Pharaoh's library and have someone read me the newest learned tomes on compounding medications, and the spells required. I'm a healer," she said with a smile.

Tuya was floored by the unusual request. "I'll talk to the Chief Scribe. He can assign one of his staff to transcribe the scrolls for you as well."

"That would be a tremendous favor, thank you. I want to speak to the Royal Physician as well, although I'm sure he'll be condescending to a mere healer." Mehyta leaned closer. "I wish to see if there are any new approaches to healing old war wounds."

Queen Ashayet called to them. "Ladies, I don't know what topic has you so enthralled. I'm glad to see you two so deep in conversation, but I was hoping Lady Mehyta might cast fortunes for us today."

Tuya thought Mehyta wasn't exactly pleased by the request, although her pretty face didn't show any sign of a frown. She rose and moved to sit beside the queen, taking a drawstring bag from her belt as she did so. "I've brought my stones, Great One. The god Shai doesn't always choose to permit me the use of them, but I'm happy to try."

Bearing in mind the vision of her future the goddess had shown her, Tuya had no desire to participate. She lingered on the edge of the eager crowd while Mehyta plucked shiny colorful stones from her bag and interpreted the meanings. Well pleased by the happy reading she received, the Royal Wife eventually singled Tuya out. "But we must have a fortune for my faithful Tuya! Tell us if she has a handsome man in her future."

Tuya tried to demur but one does not say no to the queen.

Mehyta dipped her hand into the bag then raised her empty hand into view again, flexing her fingers and frowning. "No stones come to be read." She tried again with the same result. "I believe Shai feels I've called upon him enough today," she said to the queen apologetically.

"No matter, we can continue another time," Ashayet said as servants entered the room bearing well laden trays of delicacies, followed by a trip of musicians. "The late afternoon refreshment has arrived in any case."

Tuya took a moment to speak to Mehyta. "No need to try again on my behalf. I'm content not to know my fortune. My days follow each other like ripples on the Nile—unchanging and placid."

The fortune teller eyed her. "Really? I'm not so sure, but as you wish. Unless the queen tasks me to cast the stones for you again while I'm here."

"Of course."

Many hours later, Tuya was finally free to seek her rooms, after the banquet and entertainment in honor of Pharaoh's guests ended. She took off her elegant wig and shook her own hair loose. Washing her face, she hoped no one needed her tonight and, as she changed into a simple linen shift for bed, she was barely able to keep her eyes open. Her bed was comfortable and the smooth wooden head rest carved to her specifications, so she fell asleep immediately.

Her dreams were chaotic, overlaid with a sense of dread, and she slept poorly. Indeed, she spent the last hours of the night sleeping not at all. Instead she huddled on the bench in her tiny garden, wrapped in a cloak and staring at the moon.

The next morning even her skillful hand at makeup couldn't disguise the dark circles under her eyes, and the queen remarked upon her pallor when she arrived at breakfast. "Perhaps we should order you to the countryside for a rest with no cares," Ashayet said. "You still have a house on your late stepfather's estate, as I recall."

"Yes, Great One, the deed for the property was gifted to me. I haven't been there in years. The house sits empty. But exile from court, even well meant, would be shattering to me." Even as the words left her mouth, she realized this was more honesty than she'd intended. She suppressed a worry over whether the queen was tiring of her presence. "My life is here, my joy in serving you."

Ashayet patted her hand. "And I'd be bereft without you, old friend. But see the Royal Physician if these sleep problems continue. He can prescribe a soothing herb and give you an associated spell."

"Yes, Great One. I'll seek him out today."

Satisfied, the queen moved away to chat with an ambassador's wife. Tuya took her mug of beer and her hard roll and went to sit with Mehyta.

"Did I hear you were troubled by bad dreams?" the healer asked.

"Yes." Tuya sipped the beer. "It's nothing. I'm sure my slumber tonight will be untroubled."

Mehyta set aside her own cup and plate. "I hesitated whether to broach this subject, but I discussed it with my husband. He felt I shouldn't withhold what the stones told me yesterday. Now I feel even more sure, as it may have a relationship to your dreams. Let us go onto the terrace where we may be completely private."

A sinking sensation in her stomach, Tuya followed the younger woman past the billowing draperies and outside, to the far corner of the shaded patio.

Mehyta unfastened her bag of prophecy stones. "The first time I tried to cast your fortune yesterday, it was true no stones came to my hand. The second time, I knew which stone it was by the touch and I chose not to cast shadow on the day. Before I say more, let me try again. Sometimes conditions change, altering the omens."

"I thought you said Shai had withdrawn his power yesterday."

Mehyta smiled and shook her head sadly. "A polite lie for the queen's ears. Clearly, she's extremely fond of you." She dipped her hand in the bag and brought it out again clenched into a fist. She dropped the stones onto the flat rock of the terrace. Instead of rolling, they sat where they fell. The primary stone was large, a solid gray, like granite but without veining or sparkle. "This is the one that came to my hand yesterday," Mehyta said. "I rarely see it when I cast fortunes."

Tuya licked her dry lips and swallowed. "Not a good omen?"

"As with any omen, there can be multiple meanings, but what the stone tells me is either the person has no future—"

Tuya gasped and fell back into her chair. Worse than she'd imagined, much more dire than facing years of boredom and unchanging conditions. She wasn't ready to go to the afterlife.

"Or things are unsettled. A cloud of swirling possibilities, none good. I can't give advice based on this alone. Does it have meaning for you?"

"Perhaps. I'm no seer, but I did have a vision recently, sent by the goddess Mut. I—I'd rather not speak of it."

Mehyta studied her face for a moment. "Then don't. If a goddess spoke, it was meant for you, not others."

Tuya took another rapid look at the gray stone and noticed it had two tiny companions. "What is the meaning of the second stone?"

"Now that may be a better sign." Mehyta touched her fingertip to the smaller sphere, a beautiful shimmering bronze-brown, striped like the skin of a tiger. "In this context I take it to mean you might have an ally, someone who could shift things for you, influence your future, if you choose to allow this."

Anen and his offer to leave with him came to her mind. Was she supposed to renounce her entire life and go traveling the world with her brother? Maybe she preferred the boredom and sureness the gray stone portended. "Who is this ally?"

"Impossible for me to know." Mehyta smiled apologetically. "Shai enjoys his mysteries, and I'm rarely given a specific answer. He once told me he allows humans certain choices, varying levels of influence over their path. So the possibilities realign."

"Yes, I—I've heard something similar." Tuya pointed at the third stone, a pretty turquoise. "And this?"

"It wasn't there yesterday. I believe that one to be you." Mehyta gathered up her stones and dropped them one at a time into the bag, where they fell with tiny clicking sounds. "Perhaps a time for decision is at hand." She patted Tuya on the arm. "I'm sorry it isn't a happier fortune, but I see hope flickering on the edges. Certainly the blue stone wasn't there yesterday. It's all up to you." She moved away to greet a lady who'd played senet with her the day before.

Tuya remained in her chair, hands gripping the painted lotus buds at the end of the chair arms so hard her knuckles were white. At least the vision from the goddess had been fairly clear, once she understood the symbolism. This prophecy was maddeningly vague. And frightening.

Someone touched her shoulder, and she jumped.

The other lady-in-waiting retreated. "I only came to tell you the Great One wishes us all to listen to the words of her favorite poet, who's come today with a new ode."

"Of course. I remember she promised us such a treat for today." Forcing herself to assume a pleased expression, Tuya rose and linked arms with her friend.

CHAPTER THREE

The next day the queen had arranged a cruise on the Nile on her private barge with musicians and all manner of delicacies. Tuya arrived at the royal dock with the rest of the ladies-in-waiting, stepping from their litters and queueing to board the waiting boat. She scanned the crowd for Mehyta, as the rural lady was her special assignment, but she saw her deep in conversation with another woman, so Tuya hung back. She'd slept better, thanks to the drops the physician had given her, although she had vague memories of more dreams.

As she waited, she realized one of the officers on duty at the pier was Khian. He nodded gravely as she caught his eye, and she decided to stroll over to chat for a moment. Pleased the gods had given her this opportunity to see him when there was no crisis and everyone was preoccupied with loading the queen's barge, she thought it would be a pity to miss the chance to further their acquaintance. He had been rather gallant the other night, in his high handed way.

"Good morning, my lady." He saluted as she approached his station. "You have a fine day for a sail on the Nile."

"Indeed we do, but in any event the river would hardly wish to offend the Royal Wife." He smiled, and she relaxed, good manners prompting her to add, "I wanted to thank you for your help the other night."

"Even though clearly you wished me to go to the seven hells and leave you alone with your intrigues?"

Flustered, she retreated a step. His face softened, and he followed, reaching out a hand to catch hers. "It was an honor to serve. I was frustrated you'd take such risks with your safety. Surely one as vibrant as you must be dear to the court."

She couldn't believe her ears. Had he paid her a compliment? But yes, there was a ruddy tinge under his bronzed skin and on the tips of his ears. She made a modest answer. "I'm merely one of many honored to wait on the Royal Wife."

He stood close and still had possession of her hand. "And am I forgiven for the kiss? I can't regret stealing it—your lips are very sweet."

Actually, the kiss had been memorable and had crossed Tuya's mind more than once since the moment. She was definitely attracted to Khian and the idea of being held against his hard body in the darkness for more than a quick kiss was an enticing impulse. "Are you flirting with me, sir?"

"Don't men flirt with you all the time?"

She shook her head, lowering her eyes. "Not so boldly."

He laughed. "Well, I *am* from the uncouth provinces so perhaps I speak out of turn. Forgive me?"

Tuya blinked and peeked at him through her lashes, enjoying the moment, although still a bit amazed the rural officer even knew how to flirt. "One as valiant as you can be forgiven many things."

She heard someone clear their throat ostentatiously. Seeking the source of the disapproving sound, she saw a servant standing a few feet away, bowing. "Lady Tuya, you must board the royal barge. You are among the last, and we can't keep the queen waiting."

She withdrew her hand from Khian's. "I'll be right there."

The servant bowed again and moved a little away but still lingered, clearly afraid she wouldn't be timely.

Tuya sighed. "I must go. I bid you a good day, captain."

He walked with her. "No more midnight trips into the city?"

She shook her head. "No. I've every intention of remaining in the daylight from now on."

"Are you ever allowed to attend festivals?"

Puzzled, she stopped short of the boarding ramp. "What sort of festivals?"

"The commanding general is paying for a huge dinner and ceremony in honor of Horus."

"Oh yes, Pharaoh mentioned it the other day."

"I forget your exalted status." He clenched his jaw. "Forgive me."

"What were you going to say?"

Khian seemed reluctant to answer. "Only that I've been invited and wondered if you might be there."

Flattered, she confirmed his guess. "With the Royal Wife, yes. But unmarried men and women aren't allowed to sit together at dinner in Thebes. I don't know what your customs may be in the Lower Nile provinces."

"I see. Still, it would be pleasant to know at least one other guest. Perhaps I can get assigned to night guard duty in the city again instead."

Alarmed, Tuya put her hand on his arm. "Oh no, you mustn't do that. If you were specifically invited, it would be deemed an insult to Pharaoh if you don't attend."

He laughed. "You forget I'm not making a career of the military or life at court."

"Yes, you have to get home to your planting, I recall?"

"Exactly." He seemed pleased she remembered. "But I don't wish to be disrespectful to the Great One. "

"We should make sure your memories of Thebes are pleasurable ones." She slanted a meaningful glance at him. "Perhaps I could be persuaded to show you a few of the more memorable parts of the city. A personal tour? And we could certainly converse prior to the general's dinner, earlier in the evening, when the guests mingle freely."

He raised his eyebrows and leaned closer. "I'd be honored, my lady."

"Captain, return to your post before I report you for dereliction of duty." The newcomer's voice was like a whip as he gave his order. "Lady Tuya, your absence is preventing the Royal Wife's barge from casting off. Please come with me at once."

Standing at attention, Khian saluted the senior officer, resplendent in his flowing red cloak and crisp uniform. Tuya addressed the man, with whom she had a slight acquaintance. "I'm so sorry to be a bother. I was unjustly detaining the captain from his duty by asking questions regarding his service to Pharaoh at the battle of Meribe Pass. I was curious after witnessing the gold of valor ceremony. If you'll escort me aboard the ship, I'll apologize to the Great One."

She could see from a swift glance the barge was nowhere near ready to leave, which meant she was probably not in any trouble. For some reason the officer wanted to make trouble for Khian, probably for daring to talk to a lady above his station. "Thank you for your courtesy, captain," she said to Khian before allowing the other officer to lead her away.

Safely on the barge, she hastened to check with the queen, who as she'd suspected had no idea Tuya'd lingered on the dock. The queen laughed merrily at any attempt to apologize. Relieved, Tuya sought out Mehyta, who she found at the bow, clutching the rail, an ominous greenish-tinged pallor under the makeup on her cheeks.

"Are you all right? Once we're in the main current of the Nile the barge sails as smoothly as Ra's sun boat, I assure you."

Mehyta kept her firm grip on the decorative molding. "Reassuring news indeed. I've never been on a boat before, so it's all new to me. We came overland from my husband's estate."

"Are you unwell? Should we go sit in the shade of the awning?"

Mehyta leaned closer. "I'll share a secret with you—the last time I cast the stones for myself, I found out I was going to have a child. 'Tis the morning sickness I have today, not the effect of the waves."

Repressing a flicker of jealousy, Tuya made herself respond in a happy tone. "Congratulations. May the child have a long life, prosperity, and good health."

"Thank you. My husband and I are thrilled. He hopes for an heir of course while I long for a daughter to teach my healing skills." Mehyta glanced toward the dock, from which the barge was pushing off. "I think someone wishes he were going with us today."

"What?" Tuya followed the direction of her gaze and blushed as she saw Khian watching her. She raised one hand slightly, and he reciprocated before turning away. "An acquaintance only. We should go attend the queen."

Mehyta slid her hand into her bag of prophecy stones, pulling one out far enough to see it for herself but not visible to Tuya. She let the stone slide into the depths of the pouch once more and nodded.

"What did you see?"

"Perhaps nothing. Perhaps the answer to who the tiger eye stone represented." Tilting her head, she contemplated Tuya's reaction.

"No, your interpretation's not possible," she said in genuine confusion. "We've barely met. He's from a Lower Nile nome and going home soon. To farm, I gather. What connection could there be between a lady of the court like me and a rural landholder?" Tuya thought guiltily of the undeniable physical attraction sparking between the two of them and her offer to provide him with a personal tour. She rushed on with her artless explanation. "He and his men came to my aid in the square a few nights ago, when I was late in returning from the temple. Perhaps your stones speak of that event."

Mehyta shook her head. "I see the future, not the past. Don't tax yourself over the prophecy. As we discussed before, the omens can be interpreted many ways." She walked away, within reach of the railing, her steps unsure as the barge rose and fell slightly on the Nile.

This healer sees a great deal too much. Tuya lingered a moment more. Shading her eyes, she checked the now receding dock again but couldn't pick out Khian from the crowd. There was no sign of his blue cloak. Conscious of a mild disappointment, she followed Mehyta toward the Royal Wife's pavilion in the stern. *Her interpretation of the stone is clearly in error. At most I'd share a brief dalliance with him before he departs from Thebes to go home. He's certainly pleasing to gaze upon, but he has no bearing on my future.*

Shivering a bit in a stray breeze from the river, she gathered her shawl more closely around her shoulders and hastened to join the Royal Wife.

In the evening there was another in the endless series of banquets and entertainments with which the court beguiled its leisure time during this season.

The room seemed overly warm and the oil lamps were smoky, so Tuya slipped out into the garden. There was much time before the dinner and no one would miss her. She leaned against a pillar in the cool night air and tried to relax.

A slight motion in her peripheral vision caught her attention and she spun to see none other than Captain Khian. "I think Bes or another playful god is throwing us into each other's path," he said with a soft laugh. "I came outside to escape the crowd of people talking of things I know nothing about and have no care for. And you?"

"Pretty much the same, although in my case, all the topics being discussed are things I've heard many times before. The names may change but the basics of court gossip are well established."

"If I'd known receiving gold of valor was going to mean I had to attend so many boring banquets, I might have thrown myself off the cliff at the Meribe Pass rather than defending the place," he said, tugging at the elaborate leather breastplate he wore. The gold of valor gleamed in the torchlight.

"Just be glad you don't have to wear the necklaces daily," she said, stepping closer and touching one of the golden flies with her fingertip. "They must be heavy. The Great One seeks to ensure the honor is commensurate with the deed."

"I don't mean any disrespect to Pharaoh or the honors he bestows." Khian rolled his eyes to the heavens and rubbed his jaw. "Every word is complicated in Thebes."

She patted his arm, unable to resist touching him, enjoying the feel of his strong archer's muscles under her fingers. "But as you said yourself, you're not here to make a career as a courtier. Or aspiring to become a general."

"Aye, I'm well satisfied with life as a land holder in the Jackal Nome, could I but get myself back there and stay."

She tilted her head, gazing up at him. "Is life there so much simpler there then? No banquets? Nothing to amuse a lady?"

"We have feasts and celebrations of course, but less formal in tone. As to amusing a lady such as yourself, I hope I could figure out the challenge to your satisfaction." The last was said in a lower tone, Khian giving her a meaningful glance. "I'd certainly like to try."

She licked her lips, delightfully conscious of his body so close to hers. "This garden is one of the memorable sites of which I spoke, yesterday at the queen's barge. There's a spectacular view of the Nile from the cliff, especially in the moonlight. I could show you while we're waiting for the banquet to begin."

Offering his arm, he bowed. "An invitation not to be missed."

Arm in arm they strolled away from the house, following paths illuminated by torches. Tuya'd been to this secluded spot before a time or two, but never with anyone who made her heart beat so rapidly. Her hip brushed his as they walked and she felt a tingle deep inside, a part of her that had been quiet for too long. They emerged from the garden onto the cliff and stood gazing at the Nile for a few moments.

"Lovely," he said, "but made infinitely better by your presence."

"Flatterer."

Frowning, he shook his head. "I speak the truth, Lady Tuya."

Perhaps he did, this sturdy, sensible soldier who was also a farmer and certainly no smooth-tongued courtier. Tuya'd never met a man like Khian before. His strength of character appealed to her and she was intrigued, wishing to learn more. "There's a bench," she said. "For contemplation of the river. We could sit for a few moments before we have to return to the gathering." Taking his hand, she drew him further along the cliff, to a granite bench carved in the shape of a reclining lioness curled around a seating area. "No one else is likely to come exploring at this hour." A breeze from the river below caressed her shoulders and she shivered a bit.

"You're cold?" he asked, concern in his voice.

"If we sit, I might feel warmer." She gave him a gentle push and he sat, drawing her onto his lap and into a kiss. Coaxing him closer by placing her hands on his broad shoulders and then sliding them to rest on his back, she gave a happy sigh and parted her lips.

He tasted a bit of the wine, his mouth warm and inviting, his tongue skilled in dancing with hers as he explored. She pressed against his chest, wishing it was his bare skin she touched rather than the leather breastplate. Under her bottom she felt his growing arousal and unable to resist the mischievous thought, she shifted position a bit to stoke his obvious desire.

Khian broke off the kiss, holding her close to him. "What does the poet say?" he whispered. "Waylay propriety and both be rewarded?"

Delighted and surprised he knew one of her favorite verses, she said, "Have me close in your arms, that when dawn breaks we'll be enchanted still."

He kissed her neck. "They will miss us if we're gone till dawn, my lady. And this is no proper bower for what I think we both desire."

"No," she agreed with regret although she was glad he recognized for himself they could go no further tonight. The depth of her response to him – physical and emotional – surprised her. She'd certainly traded kisses and more with handsome officers in the past, even had poetry quoted to her, but with Khian the emotions were different, deeper. Suddenly she wasn't sure she wanted to explore this connection further. Her heart was in danger and where could that possibly lead? He was a farmer bent on pursuing life in his provincial nome and she'd be left behind in Thebes, grieving his absence. Khian would be no casual court liaison for her. His touch had her entire body humming with desire and longing. She wanted him to recite more poetry to her in his deep voice—she wanted to take him by the hand and stroll and talk for hours and end up in the bedroom.

Impossible, all of it.

She had to protect her heart.

Seeming to sense her change in mood, he gently set her on her feet and rose himself, keeping his warm grip on her hand. "Perhaps we'd best walk back to the terrace." He brushed his fingertips across her cheek in a sweet caress, smoothing the strands of her wig away from her face, untangling an errant bead from its mates. "There will be other days while I remain in Thebes."

"And nights," she said, unable to stop herself.

His face set in serious lines, he nodded. "And nights, if that be your wish, my lady of moonlight."

Quoting another verse, she said, "Desire fills the cup on my side of the balance as much as it overflows on yours." She tightened her lips before the rest of the line could escape. *So allow no further delay, let us carry out our hearts' desires with each other until the night ends.* She wondered if he knew the poem and guessed from his glance at her, he must, but Khian said nothing.

Calling upon all her training as a lady of the court, she plied him with questions about his estate and the Jackal Nome and anything else safe that came to her chaotic mind and by the time they parted on the terrace to make their separate ways into the gathering, her heartbeat had slowed. As she hastened to sit with the Royal Wife at the head table, Tuya debated with herself what she truly wanted when it came to Khian. A casual affair seemed impossible to uphold – her reaction to his caresses in the moonlight and to him as a man made it clear she'd soon tumble into love with him. But what else could there be? Could she turn cold and icy to him when next they met, to protect her heart?

As the meal progressed, she tried to surreptitiously find him in the crowd, guessing he was probably seated too far away to be seen from her vantage point next to the queen. His gold of valor got him invited to this exclusive evening, but not into the inner circles of Thebes. She was disappointed and yet relieved not to encounter him again in front of others.

I'm the girl in the poem about the lover who lives on the too far side of the Nile and all the obstacles placed by the gods between them—crocodiles, rough waves, shifting currents, sandstorms.

Yet that couple was together at the end of the many verses, promised a million years of happiness by the same gods.

She drained her wine, hoping the drink might soothe her raging headache.

Two days later, she hastened to her rooms to begin preparing for the general's dinner in honor of Horus. She wanted to spend extra care on her wig and makeup, blushing a bit to realize she was hoping to make an impression on Khian, should he be in attendance. There was a small parchment scroll in the middle of her bed. Pausing in confusion, she stared at it. Heart beating faster than normal, she entertained the hopeful idea the captain had sent her a note. When she picked it up, she was disappointed the red wax seal bore no mark or cartouche. The hieroglyphics were bold, and she read the contents twice, disbelief melting into fright.

Meet me at the Inn of the Dancing Dogs near the caravan center by the tenth hour or your brother dies. Bring gold for his debts. Tell no one. Come alone and ask for Hewernef.

"Is this some kind of joke?" she said out loud, flipping the papyrus over to see if there was any other hint.

Her first instinct was to run to the queen for advice or help but then, remembering her brother was an exiled criminal, she felt she couldn't take the risk. Ashayet was fond of her but would hardly extend aid to a man her husband had sentenced for crimes.

The palace's chief scribe? No, friendly as the man was, he'd also look askance at anything to do with helping Anen. Tuya'd used up all her balance of good will at court getting her brother's original sentence commuted from death to exile. Anen wasn't supposed to be in Thebes. The question would inevitably arise how she was so sure he was in the city and in jeopardy.

Head whirling, Tuya sank down on the nearest chair, clenching her fist on the gilded leopard head of the arm rest. She fought tears and nausea. Captain Khian came to mind, but she barely knew the man, and he'd been so disapproving of her late night trip to meet Anen, without even knowing the reasons. He'd be twice as disapproving of this errand.

I promised my mother on her death bed to watch over Anen and protect him.

Tuya rose to summon Hemaka then paused. He'd been so negative about her brother – he might not support this. And what if he betrayed her to the queen or the chief scribe, thinking he was acting in her best interests? He'd never been fond of her half-brother.

She flung open the cedar chest where she'd stored the maid's apparel from her last clandestine trip into the city and changed clothing rapidly. It was daylight after all, and the area in question was highly populated, patrolled by Pharaoh's soldiers to ensure nothing interfered with the vital caravan traffic. She could safely go there, pay her brother's new debts, and leave with Anen. Take him to Behenu's house. Make it clear she was done with him if he ever set foot in Thebes again.

Her thoughts were growing disordered under the stress. Tuya opened her jewelry box and lifted out two golden bracelets, a matched set with birds and lotus flowers twining together, each embellished with pearls, coral and turquoise. She stuffed the jewelry hastily into a sack she made from one of her fringed blue scarves.

Stepping into the corridor, she took a deep breath and walked slowly toward the nearest exit from the palace, head down, trying to assume the meek, deferential air of a servant. As she escaped the grounds, scurrying past the bored guards, she realized in her haste she'd left the ransom note in her room. *Well, I'll burn it when I return.*

She moderated her pace once she was in the city proper, not wanting to attract attention, nor to arrive at her destination out of breath. She dreaded finding out who she was going to have to deal with, to buy her brother's freedom, and hoped she was capable of the task. *I'm a lady of the court. I can assert my rank if I must.* Although whoever set this scheme in motion was clearly aware of her position and also understood how her brother's past crimes could affect her standing. Once she had Anen free and safely out of the city, she might have to seek help from the queen or the chief scribe, if the kidnappers sought to blackmail her for further payments. *One problem at a time.*

The closer she got to the caravan hub, the slower her steps became. She drew aside in the shade of a palm tree and took a deep breath, suddenly terrified and unsure she could deal with whoever was holding her brother for ransom. Rushing headlong to his rescue was foolish. She chewed her lip and glanced back the way she'd come. This time there was no captain Khian come to lend his strength to her safety.

But I'm nearly there. I must see it through.

Taking a deep breath, she forced herself to walk forward, toying with pretending to be her own maid, sent on this errand. Regretfully, she decided the ruse wouldn't work. Her enemy had somehow gotten the note into her bedroom in the palace. He undoubtedly knew who she was.

The inn was ahead of her, one in a cluster of similar buildings, arrayed alongside shops selling gear and supplies a caravan master or his passengers might need for their long journeys. The air was dusty and smelled of camel dung. People pushed past her, intent on their own business. She saw a patrol of Pharaoh's guards march down the road and felt slightly reassured, taking their presence at the exact moment she needed courage as an omen from a kindly disposed god.

The inn was crowded and noisy. She edged through the open doorway and paused, only to be jostled by a pair of camel drovers. Clutching her sack tightly, she approached a serving girl. "Is there someone named Hewernef here today? I—my mistress sent me on an errand."

"Ask the master," the girl said, pointing at a man pouring streams of beer from a large clay jar into wobbly mugs. "He may have rented a room."

Tuya threaded her way through the crowd, ignoring the rude touch of a hand on her rear as she passed one table of rowdy drinkers, and others twitching at her skirt, but although she felt as if she was in a nightmare, she plowed ahead until she reached the owner's side. "Please, sir, I've come to see Hewernef, if you can direct me."

The man didn't pause in his activity. "Go out the back door, take the lane to the right, and he's waiting in a hut, third on the left."

Heart thumping, she thanked him and headed for the rear doors. It was quieter outside, and she took a shaky breath as she walked to the designated building. Tuya knocked on the wood frame of the doorway.

"Enter."

She pushed aside the reed mat hanging from the ceiling and stepped across the threshold. Two men were waiting for her and, to her surprise, one was her half-brother. "Anen! Are you all right?"

"Did you bring the gold?" he said, rising from his seat and coming to her. "If you did I'll be fine."

She looked from him to the other man, who'd also stood but remained where he was. "Is this Hewernef?"

Anen nodded, saying to the other over his shoulder, "I told you she'd come."

Feeling uneasy rather than reassured by her brother's attitude, she retreated a step. He caught her wrist and tugged her deeper into the room with such force she stumbled and fell onto the pile of pillows. "Now, now, nothing to worry about. Give me the gold."

"I thought it was for him." She pushed herself upright and got to her feet. The two men had moved together, blocking her access to the door, and she realized she was boxed in. "You seem awfully friendly with a man who's supposed to be holding you prisoner on pain of death." Tuya took a step sideways and Hewernef shifted in response.

"You see, I told you she was smart." Anen's voice was mocking.

Hewernef pointed a thick finger at him. "You talk too much. Let's get this over with."

She pulled the small dagger from its hiding spot in her belt then threw the sack holding the bracelets onto the pillows. "I'm leaving now. You can have the jewelry, but they're the last thing I'm giving you, Anen. Don't involve me in your schemes again."

Moving swiftly, Hewernef grabbed her wrist and twisted hard so she was forced to drop the knife. He clamped his other hand over her mouth and nose, easily countering her struggles to get free. Tuya clawed at him and kicked but her blows were ineffective and off target. Terror swept over her as she couldn't breathe.

"Just knock her out," Anen said with callous disregard as he bent to retrieve the sack.

Unable to believe her ears, she reached a hand to him in mute appeal, sinking to her knees still in the grasp of Hewernef, the room growing dark around her as he continued to cut off her breathing.

When she came to with a start, Tuya found herself bound hand and foot, with a gag in her mouth. She was curled up uncomfortably, and her surroundings were swaying and bobbing with a nauseating side to side motion. As the fresh scent of rushes wafted to her nostrils, she realized she was being held captive inside a large basket. The weave was tight and almost no light filtered into the stifling interior. She was terrified of throwing up while gagged so she did her best to breathe deep, praying to Mut for assistance.

Why had her half-brother had her kidnapped? The obvious answers were terrifying, but how could he think a lady of her rank and position disappearing from court wouldn't be missed? Surely men would be sent to hunt for her, once Ashayet realized her senior lady-in-waiting was gone. *Maybe Anen just wants more deben than he's been able to sweet talk from me.* Would the queen pay ransom? Would Pharaoh allow her to do so? Tuya resolved to repay the royal couple if they did, with a further tithe to the goddess Mut.

As the dizzying journey to wherever they were taking her continued, she wept, wishing she'd paid attention to Hemaka's repeated warnings about her half-brother's true character. Certainly now she no longer looked at him and saw the sweet little boy who'd so easily cajoled her out of honeyed dates and special wooden toys at the market. All his piteous stories while in Pharaoh's prison awaiting flogging and death, of how he'd never meant to do wrong, how his friends tricked him into participating in the scheme to defraud the tax collector were any of those true?

His words had torn at her heart like hungry crocodiles and drove her to plead his case to the Great One, winning him exile.

I was a fool, bound to blindness by my deathbed oath to my mother. Had their mother known the true character of the son she'd borne to her second husband, after Tuya's father died? Tuya vowed on Mut's wings she'd honored the oath to the best of her ability and was done with it now. Surely the gods would absolve her.

Her legs were cramping, but the basket held her too tightly to stretch and gain relief. A wave of relief filled her when the motion stopped and she felt the basket set down on a soft surface. Whatever was coming next might be an ordeal but at least she'd be able to see her tormentors.

No one came to release her from the container immediately, though, and she heard men's voices in the vicinity. But, no matter how hard she strained, she was unable to make out words.

As the basket was tilted sideways Tuya shrieked behind the gag. She fell out of the basket as the lid rolled away. Someone reached inside, hooking his hands under her armpits, to drag her out. She stretched her legs to ease the cramps and stared frantically about, trying to assess the situation. Three men, one of whom was Hewernef, towered over her, and she tried to glare defiantly at them. There was no sign of Anen.

One unknown man nudged her with his toe. "She has spirit but could be a common maid in those clothes. You're sure this is his sister, the queen's lady-in-waiting?"

"Aye. She's well-spoken and full of airs. Look at her wig—no maid can afford such quality." Hewernef brought her hastily made sack into view and pulled out the bracelets. "She brought these, to save him. And this pretty toy of a knife."

The man waved them away. "Keep the trinkets—you've earned them. Give the bracelets to your mistress, but I'd keep the knife well away from her. The whole caravan knows her temper when you've displeased her—no blades for her or you might find your own throat slit one night."

"In truth, knife or no, the lady was more trouble than Anen was," Hewernef said. He made a stabbing motion. "I gutted him between one step and the next. Never saw it coming. He was too eager to get here and sell you his sister for the promised reward."

Anen is dead? Angry as she was over what he'd done, she still suffered a pang of grief for the loss of her only relative. There'd be no explanation or apology this time, no way for her to understand how he could have been persuaded to join in this scheme. No chance he'd come to his senses and help her.

The master squatted next to her, touching her wig. Tuya jerked her head away from his fingers, and he laughed as he snatched the wig from her head, tossing it aside. Grabbing her chin hard with his callused fingers, he said, "I advise you to listen to me, girl. No one's going to touch you – you're not here for our pleasure, and you're not here to be sold as a slave. You've been acquired for a much nobler calling. Behave yourself, obey my orders, and you can make the journey in a measure of comfort. Not what you're used to, I'm sorry to say, but better than being carried helpless in a basket."

She glared at him as the other men laughed. He reached for the gag. "You may scream as loudly as you wish," he said. "You're far from anyone who'll help you, or care."

When he'd taken away the rag she licked her cracked lips. "Who – who are you?"

"Meketre, the caravan master." He pulled out a knife. "I'm going to cut your bonds now so hold still."

He sliced through the ropes binding her, and as the blood rushed back into her extremities she bit her lip until it bled, trying not to scream. Meketre picked her up from the carpeted floor of his tent and set her on a low divan. He issued orders to Hewernef with an impatient gesture. "The chains, quickly, before she regains full control of her limbs."

Tuya put up as much resistance as she could, flailing with her trembling arms and trying to kick, but her captors were much stronger. Soon she'd been fitted with an elaborate, lightweight set of golden manacles and shackles severely constricting her movements. She lifted her left arm to study the glittering cuff, which bore the same stylized rendition of a butterfly, wings spread, and a scorpion she'd seen on her brother's arm as a tattoo, and which Meketre also bore on his wrist.

Meketre dragged her to a set of pillows in the corner and fastened her chains to a post set there. "You'll be brought food and drink shortly," he said. "Not what you're used to at Pharaoh's table, but it'll keep you alive. While you're with us you'll sleep in my tent and travel in a covered cart behind my camel."

"I'll be missed," she said. "Pharaoh will send men to search for me. You should let me go to avoid trouble. I'd promise not to testify against you."

As he scooped up her wig and examined the beads, Meketre laughed. "If I set you free right now, pretty one, you'd wander and die unmourned in the desert. We're on the western caravan route, bound for the oasis of Kharga and lands beyond. I'll be dropping you off at a destination long before we reach Kharga, however. As to being missed, while he waited for you to show up at the inn, your late brother wrote the queen a very pretty note on your behalf, about how you'd decided to tend to family business regarding your mother's old house, and would be gone for quite some time. He sent your regrets."

Chilled, Tuya sank onto the pillows. The queen would believe the note, especially since they'd had such a recent conversation about how tired Tuya was and the fact she did still own the country house. Others would happily take on her duties and in no time it would be as if she'd never been a member of the court. This was a clever plot to ensnare her. She hoped her brother's heart had been judged harshly by the gods and the goddess Ammit had eaten it, as was her custom with the hearts of those found wanting in decency. Anen's father had been a merchant, unable to write despite his riches, but their mother was high born, so she had no doubt her half-brother had been able to compose a convincingly tasteful note. He'd been well schooled as a child, much to his father's delight. Despite her anger, she felt tears gathering, mourning the boy he'd been, not the duplicitous man who'd betrayed her.

"Where are you taking me?" she asked. "Why kidnap *me*?"

"All in good time." Meketre checked the security of the lock holding her chains and signaled to the two men. "Let's go, time to check the caravan for the night." Addressing her, he said, "Your dinner will be brought soon, and I warn you there's a guard stationed outside the tent."

A servant girl brought in several covered bowls on a tray as the men exited. Tuya tried to engage the girl in conversation, desperate to learn anything else she could about her whereabouts or her captors' ultimate intentions. The woman gave her a frightened glance and refused to speak. Tuya thanked her politely anyway.

Although she had no appetite, Tuya made herself eat. She had to keep her strength up for whatever lay ahead, and in case any opportunity to escape presented itself. She tipped a bit of the cheap beer from the mug onto the carpet as an offering to Mut and prayed as hard as she could for help.

Chapter Four

Khian was shaving with extra care since this evening was General Marnamaret's dinner in tribute to Horus the Falcon god. He hummed a popular tune he'd been hearing in the marketplace and wondered how difficult it would be to get Lady Tuya aside for more private conversation. She was so lovely and seemed sweet-natured in a way that appealed to him.

Peering into the shiny surface of the bronze plate on his wall serving as a mirror, he shook his head. "She's not for the likes of you, rural farmer. Too high born, too used to being a pampered lady at court." But an enjoyable diversion while he was posted here for the remainder of his service time. He'd have to guard his heart—Tuya crept into his thoughts the way the desert breeze worked its way through shuttered windows.

The soldier in charge of orderly duty in the communal officers' barracks knocked on the door jamb and saluted. "You have a visitor, sir."

Before he could get his hopes up perhaps Tuya had done such an improper thing as to step inside the barracks to see him, her elderly servant Hemaka rushed past the guard. His face was flushed, he was breathing hard, and he clutched a crumpled papyrus in one hand. "She needs help," he said, barely able to articulate the words.

Khian thanked the guard and dismissed the man as he guided the elderly servant to the narrow bed to sit. He rushed to get the waterskin and urged Hemaka to drink. "Catch your breath before you try to share news. May I see this?" Gently, he removed the damp papyrus from the servant's clenched fingers, smoothed it out on his bedside table and read it twice. Dread settled in his gut. *Foolish, impulsive woman—she's undoubtedly in deep trouble.* "This is the half-brother you told me about? The one she went to meet the night I accompanied you to the inn?"

Hemaka set aside the waterskin. "The same ruffian. She fails to see who he really is, what he's become as a man. For all I know, he sent this note himself, colluding in a plot with his cronies to further enrich himself. But she shouldn't be in an area like the caravan hub alone, masquerading as a servant girl, carrying gold."

"On that we agree. You're sure she took something of value with her?"

Hemaka nodded. "Her favorite pair of matching arm bands are missing. And she has a knife, a pretty thing with a cat's head at the hilt. It was a gift from—from one of her close friends in the past. She hates knives, but if she took it she must have been expecting things not to go well."

"How long since she—"

The old man shook his head. "I don't know. Certainly after the noon meal. But she should be in her room right now and nearly ready to accompany the queen to the dinner General Marnamaret is giving. And there's no sign of her."

"This is a mess," Khian said. "Why come to me and not the queen? Or the captain of the palace guard?"

"You – you seem to like her." Hemaka hung his head. "I was hoping you'd help me get her back to the palace without anyone else knowing she's dealing with her half-brother. I don't think she understands the trouble she'll be in. The Royal Wife can only protect her so far."

Khian looked at the note again and grabbed his blue cloak from the peg beside the door. "She may be in much worse trouble than you're imagining. We should go immediately."

On the way out of the barracks, he pulled his second-in-command of the company from the Jackal Nome and gave him quick orders about the night's patrolling. On an impulse, he took two of his soldiers with him. The trip was at least partly official, since a lady of the court was in peril. Then he and Hemaka made their way to the bustling area of Thebes where the caravans arrived and departed. Khian had no trouble finding the inn and receiving terse directions to the small house down the road.

Sword in hand, he burst through the door, Hemaka and the two soldiers on his heels. The room was empty, save for Anen's lifeless body, slumped over on the pillows, blood congealing around him. At first Khian believed there was no sign of Tuya's presence, but then a colorful bead in the corner of the room attracted his attention. Picking it up, he examined the trinket closely. "From her wig. I remember the way the coral was cunningly set into the stones. Only Tuya would masquerade as a maid yet wear her fine wig."

"What do we do now?" Hemaka was trembling. "Where can they have taken her?"

"I'm setting my men to guard this house. You stay here with them and make sure no one touches anything. I'm going to the palace, to report this."

Getting an audience with the Royal Wife proved difficult. The commander of the palace guard was highly resistant to the idea, even though Khian emphasized repeatedly he had strong evidence to believe a lady-in-waiting was in danger. Khian grew more and more impatient as he pled his case for access to the Royal Wife. *I should have tried talking to her at the banquet instead.* His rural roots showing again. It hadn't occurred to him how many layers of bureaucracy stood between him and executing his duty.

As Khian teetered on the ragged edge of losing his temper the Chief Scribe entered the room, took one look at the two of them and raised his eyebrows. "It seems I'm just in time."

Edekh was an imposing figure who could be taken for royalty himself, if one wasn't well versed in how the palace ran. He took the chair the commander had been sitting in and steepled his fingers as he surveyed Khian standing at attention.

"I'm sorry to ask you to repeat yourself when you're obviously feeling under duress, Captain Khian," he said, quite kindly. "But what's this all about?"

Khian gritted his teeth, praying to the gods for patience. "Lady Tuya had a half-brother who was a convicted criminal under sentence of exile," he said, deciding he might as well lay out all the facts to Edekh or he stood no chance of making his case for help to any higher authorities. "Today she received an alarming note containing a threat to his life. In her agitation, she appears to have gone to meet the author of the note, unwisely taking with her a quantity of her own gold jewelry. Her elderly servant reached out to me, and we hastened to the appointed meeting place, where we found signs of a struggle, the brother's corpse, and no sign of Lady Tuya. I left two of my troops guarding the spot and hurried here to request assistance."

Edekh drummed his fingers on the table, brown furrowed in a frown as if he was sorting through the various facts. "You've seen this note?"

"Yes, sir."

"And there was no threat made to Pharaoh or the Royal Wife."

"No, my lord."

Edekh rose. "Come, we'll go apprise the queen of the situation. She has been told you're here, requesting an audience on a matter to do with Lady Tuya."

Khian followed the Chief Scribe through the corridors to the queen's apartments, where they were admitted with no questions asked. Ashayet, dressed in an elegantly pleated gown and a gleaming golden collar with matching earrings, ready for the general's dinner, was seated in a gilded chair beside a small fountain. Her face, although expertly made up, appeared tired, with lines around her green-accented eyes. Edekh bowed, and Khian saluted.

"What have you learned?" the queen asked.

Edekh bade Khian repeat his tale, which he did, concisely.

"I can add to this account," she said, surprising them both. She took a papyrus scroll from a box on the table beside her. "I received this note a few hours ago, purporting to be from Tuya, but I know she didn't write it. Adding your news to this strange note I was sent, I fear greatly for her."

Khian controlled his desire to snatch the scroll and read it. Unsure of court protocols and etiquette, he had to tread carefully here in the presence of the Royal Wife. Edekh took the note, read it, raised one eyebrow and offered it to Khian. Amazed by the deference being shown to him, Khian read it before the scribe changed his mind.

To my greatly beloved and revered Queen,

It is with regret I must ask leave to withdraw from the radiance of your company for a time and take care of family matters having to do with my mother's house on the old family estate...

The note contained lines of fulsome praise for the queen and apologetic excuses, but nothing else of substance. Khian thought it didn't sound like any conversation he'd ever had with Tuya, but what did he know of proper forms for sending a queen notes? He gave the papyrus to Edekh, who then asked the question he himself was burning to voice.

"Might I ask how you know the note was not from Tuya, Your Majesty?"

"I've known her since we were girls," the queen said, "And she never could master writing her symbols with any precision. She was too impatient." She took the note and pointed out several examples of beautifully formed hieroglyphics. "Whoever wrote this had a much finer hand than my poor Tuya. More schooling perhaps. Besides, the tone is not at all like her, not like how we spoke to each other in private."

The door at the rear of the room, which only Pharaoh could use, opened and the Great One himself walked in. "I received your message," he said to his wife. Eyebrow raised, he addressed Edekh. "What's the crisis?"

After he'd been given the facts as they were known, Nat-re-Akhte turned his attention to Khian. "What fate do you believe has fallen Lady Tuya?"

"I think she's been kidnapped, probably smuggled out of Thebes with a caravan departing today."

"And your logic?"

"This set up smacks of more than thugs seeking gold in exchange for Anen's life, or even a rash adversary deciding in the heat of the moment to abduct the lady and kill the brother. I'm worried about Tuya," he said more honestly than he intended, but the time being lost while she was taken further away from help frustrated him no end. "And I'm concerned there may be larger stakes here since the matter touches your court. If I may be so bold, Great One."

Pharaoh and Edekh exchanged glances. "A good summary," the ruler said. "Can you drive a chariot, captain?"

"Sir?"

"If I send you to track our missing lady, you must move with all speed."

"I'm not trained as a combat charioteer but yes, I've driven teams."

"Good. My chief scribe will assign the right man to help you investigate this occurrence and pursue the trail wherever it may lead. You act in my name and with my authority in this matter, captain." He gave Ashayet a fond glance. "I wish to set my wife's mind at rest regarding her lady-in-waiting. And as you're already involved in the matter, and have no other pressing, regular duties in Thebes, I think it best you take charge. " He held out one hand and his queen rose from her chair to join him. "We should be going to the banquet. Marnamaret will have had to make the guests wait on our pleasure, and I don't wish the god Horus to take insult from our late arrival."

Ashayet's maids, who'd been silent observers of the meeting, smoothly handed her an ostrich feather fan and her shawl, and the royal couple moved to the main door, where the guards saluted and followed the Great Ones from the room.

Pausing in the doorway, the queen looked over her shoulder. "Bring my friend safely home, captain." Worrying at her lower lip, she allowed Pharaoh to lead her away.

The chief scribe moved forward. "Captain, you have the air of a man who's been caught in a dust devil—a bit dazed." He slapped Khian on the back. "We should adjourn to my office. I'll have the person Pharaoh spoke of summoned, and the two of you can take the promised chariot to the scene of the crime."

Any other time Khian would have been interested in this unusual view of the inner areas of the palace, but his worry for Tuya was at the forefront of his mind. Edekh's office was a large, airy chamber, with five scribe's desks in the outer chamber. His assistants worked there even now at this late hour. A large desk with gazelle feet filled his inner office, paired with a chair carved in intricate scenes of gazelles leaping and frolicking next to a river full of fish. He felt a bit like those carved antelopes in that moment, trapped, unable to move, unable to be *doing*. Every minute of delay meant Tuya was getting farther and farther away. And the chances of rescuing her grew smaller and smaller.

The scribe went to an ebony side table and poured himself a mug of beer. "Would you care for a drink, captain?"

"Very kind of you, sir." He took the proffered drink and wet his lips. Unable to stand in one spot, he wandered to a wall and examined the elaborate wall paintings while Edekh gave orders to underlings behind him. *Too long, too long*. Everything was taking so damned long.

"Officer Nikare has arrived," a servant announced.

"Send him in." Edekh seated himself behind the desk.

Taking his cue from the Chief Scribe, Khian set his mug on the serving table and went to stand at parade rest to the side of the desk.

The newcomer was tall and well-muscled, as if he wrestled for his deben. He wore a kilt and tunic of good quality and had leather wristbands decorated with inlaid gold thread. His head was bald. "You sent for me, my lord?"

"Captain Khian, meet Officer Nikare, one of the top men in Pharaoh's police force which patrols the city of Thebes. The Medjai deal with civil matters such as murders and kidnappings."

"I thought the army kept order in Thebes," Khian said as he nodded to Nikare.

"And so it does," the Medjai said cheerfully. "But there's order of more than one kind. The military understands the use of force. My colleagues and I employ more subtle means of uncovering the Great One Ma'at's truth and making sure her precepts are followed in Pharaoh's city. We ensure wrongs don't go unpunished or uncorrected."

Khian didn't feel he'd gotten much enlightenment from the answer.

Edekh cleared his throat. "Pharaoh has assigned the two of you to this matter of the kidnapping of Lady Tuya and the murder of her half-brother Anen. He's invoking the military and the civil authorities to maximize the chance of retrieving the lady."

Nikare shifted at the murdered man's name and Khian cast him a sidelong glance. Clearly, the Medjai had some prior knowledge of Tuya's brother.

"The Great One has set no time frame, no parameters. You are to have the use of a royal war chariot and one team of horses, and may draw upon the royal treasury to a limited degree, as necessary." The scribe gave them a stern frown. "Justification will be required for any major expenditures."

Nikare laughed, a deep booming sound. "I will swear before the gods my men had to buy all that wine in order to convince the smuggler we were legitimate."

"Yes, but the dancers were an unnecessary extra." Shaking his head at what was apparently an old bone of contention between them, Edekh continued, "I think once you have followed all the possibilities and exhausted the trails, Pharaoh will be content."

Khian's heart sank. *He doesn't think we're going to find her. Or not alive anyway.*

As if reading Khian's mind, Edekh said, "Of course, the preferred outcome is the return of the lady in question to the queen's side, unharmed."

"Of course." Nikare's agreement was smooth.

"We waste time talking," Khian said, his frustration finally breaking through.

"I'll release you to charge off on the mission in a moment, impatient one. I don't expect regular reports, considering your mission may take you anywhere in the Black Lands or outside of them." He handed them each a small papyrus. "Authority to call upon Pharaoh's resources, if you need soldiers or anything else."

"My men, the company I brought from the Jackal Nome," Khian said, "I've left my second-in-command in charge. Should I fail to complete this new mission in time, Pharaoh will allow them to sail home when our tour of duty ends, won't he? We have to get to the planting. The growing season has a specific time frame in our province."

Edekh suppressed laughter. "Your concern does you honor, captain. I'll personally ensure the company is allowed to leave Thebes on time. But, honestly, I expect you'll resolve this matter before then. One way or the other. May the gods go with you. Dismissed."

Khian saluted, and the two men left the chief scribe's office together. A scribe offered to escort them to the courtyard where the chariot would be waiting.

"I need to see the crime scene," Nikare said. "There will be various threads to run down from there."

"I left two of my men and the lady's servant guarding the hut." Khian paused at the threshold of the courtyard, admiring the team of spirited black horses hitched to an impressively large war chariot. Despite the urgency of making progress on finding Tuya, he took a deep breath to calm his energy and walked to the horses' heads. He allowed them to sniff his hand, becoming acquainted with them so they'd be more responsive to his driving. "What are their names?" he asked the groom.

"Bebi and Dagi," the man said.

Khian continued his examination, pleased to find both horses sound and ready to run. "I promise to take good care of your fine steeds."

"Thank you, sir." He handed Khian the reins, bowed and retreated.

"Shall we?" Khian stepped into the chariot basket, pleased at how well balanced it was on the two wheels. He appreciated the stock of arrows and spears in the quivers, and the fine bow resting on two pegs. Nikare joined him as the gate was swung open by the guards, and Khian set the team to a trot, heading into the city streets. He hadn't driven a chariot in several years, not being assigned to that duty in the army, but he hadn't lost his skill and the crowds parted as his vehicle approached.

They arrived at the caravan hub in fairly short order, and Khian drew the team to a halt in front of the small hut where Tuya had last been seen. He put one of his soldiers in charge of the horses before pausing to speak with Hemaka. "Pharaoh has assigned me to work with the investigator and try to find Tuya," he said.

The old man wept. "I fear she's lost to us forever. I fear what's being done to her even now."

And I. But Khian patted the older man's shoulder. "Whoever is behind this plot expended a lot of effort to lure her here. I hope whatever their ultimate plan is she's being treated well. We have time."

"You really think so?"

"Yes." He made his answer firm. "I'm sure the investigator will want to talk to you then I'll drive you to the palace when we're done."

"Won't you have to be pursuing whoever has my lady? I can make my own way to the palace."

"I promise you, if I have any slightest glimmer where to charge off to, or the Medjai uncovers a clue, I'll waste no time." He laid his hand on Hemaka's shoulder for a moment. "No one feels the urgency of this matter more than I—you should have seen me at the palace, demanding to speak to someone in authority, roaring like a lion at the scribes and officers. Thank the gods the Chief Scribe eventually took notice. But it'll be dark soon and I can't take a chariot into the desert at night without a clear destination and more moonlight than the goddess Nuit will grant tonight. Have you eaten or drunk anything?"

Hemaka shook his head. Khian made him sit in the shade beside the hut and sent the second soldier running to buy bread and beer for the old man. Then he went inside the hut to join Nikare. The stench was astounding.

"You seemed to react when Anen's name was mentioned," Khian said as he watched Nikare examining the body.

"We've been aware of him since he was caught in the tax evasion scheme. Nothing particular that he was involved in recently to our knowledge." Nikare pointed at the corpse's wrist. "See this tattoo? The butterfly and scorpion? My commanders think there may be significance to this symbol which as yet escapes our grasp. We've found it on several criminals in the last year. He was killed with a single stab wound. My guess is he trusted whoever was here with him, probably set his half-sister up to be taken, and didn't realize he'd outlived his usefulness. How did you know him?"

Khian was glad he'd no secrets to hide. Nikare's gaze was penetrating, his hazel eyes sharp and assessing as he listened closely to what Khian had to say. "I never met the man. I escorted his sister to an ill-advised late night meeting which I was later informed by Hemaka had been with her half-brother."

"Ah yes, the servant. I need to ask him a few questions."

"He's waiting outside." Khian hesitated. "He's elderly and frail."

Nikare's eyebrows rose. "You worry I'll beat him for answers? Of course the old ones among us must be respected—he'll come to no harm. But Pharaoh and my commanders are concerned that notes were left inside the palace by persons unknown, especially the scroll sent to the Royal Wife. Any light the servant can shed on the issue will be helpful." He rose, dusting his hands off. "I'm done in here. We can go outside."

"What'll happen to the body?"

Nikare shrugged. "A common criminal, killed by other criminals. The body will be tossed into a mass unmarked grave. His ka will wander forever because none will do him honor or remember his name." It seemed he was done with the subject of Anen.

Khian was surprised to find four more Medjai waiting for them outside the hut. Nikare excused himself and stepped away to give orders sending his men moving rapidly in separate directions. When Nikare rejoined him, Khian asked, "Now what? I've never been a part of anything like this, trying to solve a crime. My interest is to find Tuya and get her home, gods willing."

"Yes, you've made your own goal clear." Nikare flashed an easy grin. "My men go to ask many questions, at the inn, at the caravan gathering place, elsewhere I won't bore you with. I need to talk to Hemaka then you can take him back to the palace as you promised. I won't need you tonight."

Khian's temper flared at this easy dismissal. "We're assigned to this together."

"But we each have our particular skills to bring to bear." Nikare was as unruffled as ever. "You aren't familiar with Thebes in general, much less with the people my men and I need to find and talk to. When we're riding in that fine chariot on whatever trail we decide to follow, then you'll be in charge and certainly if we have to do battle to retrieve our missing lady of the court, I'll look to you and your sword. Or the bow and arrow. I'm no soldier." He slapped Khian's arm. "I'll meet you at the officers' barracks at two hours past dawn and, as we breakfast, I'll brief you on what we've learned between now and then. Together we'll decide on the next move, agreed?"

Khian studied the setting sun. As he'd told Hemaka gloomily a bit earlier, there was no way to set off after Tuya tonight and no hint what direction to even point his horses. Much as he hated to incur more delay, Nikare was right. "Tomorrow—"

"Were I a betting man, I'd wager tomorrow will see us jouncing along in the chariot, long gone from Thebes. I'm sure we both suspect she was taken by caravan, or else why commit the crime on the outskirts of the primary travel oasis?"

Khian sighed in relief that the man felt as he did, but Nikare's next words surprised him. "On the other hand, this could be a clever ruse designed to send us in the wrong direction. Perhaps the lady remains in Thebes, and there's no connection with the caravan trade at all. I must consider all the possibilities and gather what shreds of truth there may be to guide our choice. I think Lady Tuya only has one chance, if any, and we must do our best to pick the correct set of moves. Now, the servant."

Khian's opinion of the Medjai was quite a bit higher after the explanatory speech. He stood by while Nikare led Hemaka through an easy discussion of events, starting with Tuya's clandestine meeting with her half-brother at the old nursemaid's house the week before. As far as Khian could judge, no new facts were uncovered during the interrogation, but it was thorough. Khian then said good night to his new partner, loaded Hemaka into the chariot and slowly drove to the palace, his two soldiers keeping pace behind them.

"Will you be all right?" he asked Hemaka as the soldiers helped him down from the chariot. "Should I ask the guards to summon anyone to help you?"

"I'll be fine. I have friends in the servant quarters who'll watch over me tonight. Tomorrow I'll clean up the mess in the lady's chambers then I'll pray for your success in finding her." Hemaka reached up to grasp Khian's wrist. "Thank you, captain, and may the gods lend you wings."

"I'll find her," Khian swore. "You'll be reunited."

Khian was bone tired, not so much from physical exertions, but the tension of the entire day, including personal conversation with Pharaoh and the Royal Wife. He wondered idly how the banquet had gone and if Horus had been pleased by the event in his honor. He wished he and Tuya had been there. Suddenly an official, formal boring banquet seemed like the most alluring event in all of Egypt, if only she were safely there at this hour.

As he took the chariot to the stables and supervised the servants unhitching the horses, grooming and feeding them, he wanted to pray, but to which of the Great Ones? Tuya was a priestess of Mut, but a warrior such as himself didn't normally pray to the goddess.

But would his own Jackal God take any interest in a lost noblewoman, who had no connection to him? Unlikely. Anubis had loftier concerns.

Restless, he paced through the stables as he pondered recent events in his mind. Khian had wanted to know so much more about Tuya, to spend delicious hours talking about everything and nothing, to hold her, touch her—all things that might never happen. He realized he'd been well on his way to falling in love with her, given any encouragement at all. A dangerous prospect when he needed a clear head to decide how best to find her. *If she's even alive…*Determinedly, he thrust away the bleak thought. He paused and found himself in an unfamiliar corner of the stables. Frustrated, he had to take a moment to orient himself in the unfamiliar passages of the place before he found his way again.

Khian took himself to the commissary for a belated dinner. His second-in-command arrived shortly, and he briefed the man on his special assignment, leaving out most of the details. His loyal lieutenant was happy for him to have this chance to shine in Pharaoh's eyes if the assignment went well. They discussed the plans for his own company to carry out its assigned duties in Thebes in Khian's absence.

"The company is yours now," Khian said, clapping his friend on the shoulder. "The men respect you and will take your orders. Don't let these local Theban officers bully you or them. Stand up for yourself and the Jackal Nome. I'll be back as soon as I can."

"And we'll sail home to our sweethearts and the planting," his friend said with a contented smile. "Done with war and adventuring."

Khian reckoned his days of adventure were just beginning.

Alone in his own room at last, Khian undressed and went straight to sleep. He'd disciplined himself to fall asleep rapidly each night, as a tired soldier couldn't fight at his peak.

In his dreams he found himself standing in the desert at night, staring off to the west, feeling a pull and a yearning in his heart that he didn't understand. Something made a slight sound to his right, and he pivoted to see what at first he thought was a large white bird, its feathers glowing. Even as he stood there staring the creature morphed into a beautiful woman between one moment and the next.

She was taller than he, with a serene, heart-shaped face of utmost beauty. Her dress, which had been a glowing white linen shift, elegantly pleated, became bright red, with blue stripes at the hem. Faintly, the scent of the blue lotus came to his nostrils as she stepped to his side, also facing the desert. She glanced at him. "I meant you to be her chance for change or hoped so at any rate. But one must be careful what one asks for, even a Great One such as me. Once events were set in motion, other players stepped in to reach for my game piece, and now my poor Tuya is in grave danger. I fear I was quite rude to Shai and demanded he readjust her fortune to what I'd originally meant it to be, but he laughed and said I must yield to the whims of Fate."

"I'll find her, Great One," he said, greatly daring in addressing a goddess, but speaking from the heart.

She shook her head, which set the golden beads in her lustrous wig to chiming. "The desert is vast and trackless. I'll order my children to help as much as they can, for they see much from the sky. Watch for them."

She set her fingers on his arm, and his entire body tingled with her power. "I'm not a goddess of war and soldiers, yet if I'm to help my priestess, I must step into an unaccustomed role. Will you be my champion in this, Khian of the Jackal Nome? Tuya's champion?"

"You ask of me what I've already pledged Pharaoh to accomplish, my lady." But he nodded solemnly. "I'm honored to assist you."

"Good. Pharaoh sees much merit in you, which gives me hope."

A flight of golden flies, shaped like the gold of valor he'd received only a few short weeks ago from Pharaoh's hand, buzzed and flew a circular pattern around him before arrowing across the desert and disappearing from view. Khian felt dizzy, from the intense perfume and the awe of being in the presence of a goddess. He clenched his fists and stood straighter, trying to concentrate.

"Yet you are but human," she said in a sad voice, "and as such cannot prevail against some foes. I've pleaded for help from one who fights such battles, and he has said he'll send a warrior to your side. Only one – this matter of my priestess isn't of pressing import to Egypt's fate – but I see the potential for future problems and the Lord of the Sacred Land agrees."

Anubis, she speaks of Anubis. Despite his family's ties to the jackal god, Khian suffered the sting of momentary terror. Hard enough to have a goddess sharing her concerns with him, but the idea of having Anubis pay direct attention to him was so outside his wildest imagining Khian could barely hold the idea.

"Go with my blessing, and bring her home. This is my command." The goddess faded, as if she'd been no more than a mirage in the desert.

Khian sat up straight in his bed with a gasp, hand to his heart as if saluting a superior officer. Throat parched, he reached for his waterskin on the table, and his hand brushed something soft. With a pounding heart, he picked up the white feather, which glowed in the moonlight, its quill gleaming gold. As he watched, the feather shrank and changed until it was a tiny amulet bead, strung on a fine black leather cord. Hastily, he fastened the thong on his left wrist, where the feather lay against his skin. Pride at wearing a symbol of Mut, the World-Mother, suffused his mind and heart, since she'd named him her champion. As the goddess had said, she was no patron of war or soldiers but nonetheless it seemed there was a battle of unusual nature in the offing. Since the prize at the center of the conflict was Tuya he wouldn't shirk the challenge.

CHAPTER FIVE

In the morning, he met Nikare in the officers' commissary as promised, and they swiftly breakfasted on bread and beer. "What have you learned?" Khian asked.

"I think we'll be chasing a caravan later today," the police officer said as he dipped his bread into yogurt. "My men found witnesses who watched two men carry an unusually large covered basket from the hut yesterday, place it in a donkey cart, and drive off into the oasis."

"Tuya was inside the basket?"

Face grave, Nikare nodded. "I believe so. We've reached a dead end with the innkeeper. He was paid in advance, in gold, for the use of the hut for several days, and he asked no questions. He and his servant girl confirmed a woman matching the Lady Tuya's description came to the inn asking for a man named Hewernef. They sent her to the hut as agreed upon with their temporary tenant."

"Who is this Hewernef?"

"We've not run across him before, at least not by that name. To be sure, I had the scribes at the Medjai library double check the records. We have a physical description now, thanks to the staff at the Dancing Dogs – I'll know the man if we see him. An interesting detail." Nikare drank from the mug while Khian sat impatiently. "The innkeeper mentioned noticing Hewernef sported an unusual tattoo."

"Let me guess—a butterfly and a scorpion?"

"Indeed." Nikare took another slow drink. "It may be a coincidence, but I rather think not. We have agents digging deeper into what Anen may have been doing in Thebes besides having tender reunions with his old nursemaid and his half-sister. But our primary concern, as charged by Pharaoh himself, is to find Lady Tuya, I think it's time we took to the road. "

"I'll order the chariot made ready, and we should draw supplies from the stores here," Khian said. "Water, a few days' provisions. The best maps available for the caravan routes."

"Of course we can stop at the oases along the way as does any traveler but at it's very likely we might find ourselves off the beaten path before the quest is done, depending where this all leads us. My suggestion is we portray ourselves as special inspectors, sent by Pharaoh to do random spot checks of caravans for proper payment of tax duties. He does send such teams on occasion." Nikare grinned.

"Really?"

"I believe in point of fact the Chief Scribe's administration oversees the details but yes, taxes on goods flowing in and out of the Black Lands are an important funding source for the government. Where do you think your military pay comes from?" Nikare gave him an amused glance. "The gods don't rain deben from the sky."

"I never thought much about it at all," Khian admitted. "I pay my taxes and my tithes on the crops I grow and the cattle I raise on my lands—"

"As a proper law abiding citizen who upholds the principles of ma'at should. Unfortunately not all residents of the Black Lands are as devoted." Nikare shook his head in mock sadness. "But it's a good cover for what we're really hunting, and it won't raise any special alarm for whoever may have kidnapped the lady. I recommend you let me take the lead when we're dealing with the caravan masters."

"Where do we start?" Khian asked as they left the dining hall and headed for the stables.

"At the caravan hub. One of my men will meet us there with information on which masters took their trains out the day of the murder."

"Can't we narrow the list to only those leaving later in the day?"

"Unfortunately no. The donkey cart could have been going to catch up to a caravan already on the move. Once we have a list of travelers we'll have to throw the gaming sticks and decide who to pursue. If we're lucky, if the gods favor us, all the departures will have taken the same road, and we can run them down one by one."

But the gods showed little sign of favoring them, Khian mused with dismay, as he listened to Nikare's associate list the five caravans that had departed from Thebes during the relevant time frame.

"So, it seems we have a choice to make." The Medjai said, after he'd thanked his man and sent him off to investigate other matters. He leaned on the chariot and ticked points off one by one on his fingers. "Two caravans traveling to the west to Kharga and beyond. One heading to the east, one to the north and one to the south. I think we can write off the ones headed for Kharga and the south."

"Why?" Khian thought he felt a tingling in the wrist which bore the feather amulet. He raised his eyes to the cloud-free, blue bowl of the sky, but saw no birds.

"There has to be more to this than simply kidnapping a beautiful highborn woman to be sold in a foreign market as a concubine. No one is going to concoct such an elaborate plot to reach inside Pharaoh's court, inside his very palace, for a woman to enslave. Lady Tuya is many things, all special and unique I'm sure, but not a legendary beauty such as the ancient Queen Nefertiti who all men might long to possess. Is my judgment correct?"

"She's a lovely woman with a sweet personality," Khian said, bristling instinctively on Lady Tuya's behalf before making a placating gesture with one hand. "I see your point, but why does this rule out the western and southern routes?"

"Nowhere to sell such a rare commodity at a high enough profit. Now the caravan going north on the other hand, might be carrying her to the sea, to be shipped off to one of Pharaoh's enemies, someone who looks covetously on Egypt's riches and hopes to use Lady Tuya's status as a bargaining chip, or to wring information from her. She might not have such knowledge, but a non-Egyptian might well believe as a confidant of the queen's she would be privy to secrets. Anen could have exaggerated her importance. And under torture from a skilled interrogator, she might actually know more about how the court operates than we think."

Nauseous and enraged simultaneously, Khian took violent objection to the idea of the delicate woman being subjected to abuse and torture in pursuit of secrets she didn't possess. *I can't allow her to suffer such a fate.*

"And, as a further point, we know Anen had spent time in Minos and other countries in the area. He was obviously a key part of this plot to lure Tuya to where she could be easily taken. I wonder if the original plan was to seize her at the nursemaid's home? Certainly he could have had this Hewernef or others waiting in the inn there, but your presence might have deterred them." Nikare patted the flank of the horse nearest to him. "Of course these arguments also support us following the caravan which headed east, except there we have no information about Anen having traveled into our enemies' realms."

Khian checked the harness, mostly to have something to do with his hands while he considered the conflicting options. "We cannot chase all the caravans."

"No."

"And Pharaoh made it plain he wasn't assigning anyone else to the task."

"Agreed."

"So her life rests on us making the right choice, and if we pick the wrong road, she'll be gone or dead. There'll be no time for us to backtrack hundreds of miles and chase down other caravans." He ran his hand down the left horse's leg and checked the hoof as the animal had seemed to favor it a bit, but he found nothing to worry him.

North seemed to be the right destination, based on all the facts, but the obvious answer didn't sit right with him. He straightened, prepared to agree anyway.

The hoarse shriek of a bird above drew his eyes to the sky again. A flock of vultures circled just outside the oasis, to the west. As he shaded his eyes to watch, a large white vulture flew to the west, the rest of the birds following in a tight V formation. The amulet on his wrist grew hot against his pulse point. Unfastening the leather reins, he ran to the rear of the chariot and jumped in. "West, we go west."

Nikare made a last minute leap as the chariot rolled past him, gathering speed under Khian's encouragement to the team. Hanging onto the rail, he said, "What supports your sudden decision?"

"The birds," Khian said. "An omen, I feel sure." He glanced at Nikare. "Lady Tuya is a priestess of the Great One Mut."

"And you believe the goddess takes a personal interest in this case?"

"I'm sure of it."

Nikare gave a good-natured laugh. "Well, as we're already moving out, I'm hardly going to dispute you."

Tuya cried herself to sleep the first night, forced by the chains to sleep in an awkward position. Meketre came in late, smelling of beer, and approached her unsteadily. She tensed and prepared to offer what futile resistance she could, but he merely checked the soundness of the lock holding her before falling onto his own sleeping mat. Soon he was snoring.

She slept fitfully the rest of the night. In the morning, humiliation waited as Meketre loosened her chains from the post and took her outside to the private areas to take care of her morning needs, standing and watching her. It was hard to move in the chains and, light though they were, the cuffs chafed her skin at the wrists and ankles.

Back in the tent, tethered to the post, she found a bowl of gruel, which apparently the servant girl had brought for her, and a mug of beer. She forced herself to eat the unappetizing mush and contemplated escape.

They had guards at the oases, didn't they? If she could attract the attention of one, plead her case, make a scene…

Meketre strolled in, patting his gut with satisfaction, having apparently break-fasted on offerings more inspiring than what she'd been given. He tossed her a hard roll, which she caught with both hands. "No more baskets," he said. "Today you ride in style in the donkey cart. Not as nice as the litters you were used to in Thebes but an improvement in status."

The servant girl came in, eyes downcast, carrying a basin of water and several cloths.

"But first you need to wash your face. My girl pointed out what a mess you've become, all that elegant malachite and kohl smearing with your tears. You'll attract attention for the ruined countenance alone. Be quick for we leave in a few minutes."

He left the tent. Tuya bathed her face and the rest of herself as rapidly as she could, feeling a bit refreshed. The water was cold, though, and there were no scrubbing sands.

"How do I look?" she asked the other girl.

Taking a quick glance, the woman picked up the bowl and cloths and prepared to leave.

Tuya laid a hand on her hers. "I understand why you can't speak to me, or don't dare, but I want you to know how much I appreciate your consideration. I'm grateful. It makes the situation a little more bearable to know there's a sympathetic woman nearby, that I'm not just alone with Meketre and his henchmen."

"My name is Tentopet," the girl whispered. "I'm sorry for the evil my master has brought to you."

Tuya heard heavy footsteps approaching and released her hold on the servant, who scurried out of the tent with the basin, barely missing Meketre.

He escorted Tuya outside, one proprietary hand clamped around her elbow, and lifted her into the waiting cart. The cart featured a thatched cover, with fabric stitched at either end that could be closed to obscure the inside. A driver waited next to the braying donkey.

"Take good care of our prized guest," she heard Meketre say while she struggled to find a comfortable position on the unforgiving wooden floor of the small conveyance. The cart swayed as the driver mounted the front then jerked into motion as the caravan commenced its long journey for the day.

The interior was dim, but she found a full waterskin, and she still had the hard roll. She wanted to peek out the back of the cart but found it'd been laced firmly shut, and she didn't dare approach the front. She feared Meketre would react badly to any attempt on her part to influence the driver to help her.

As she braced herself against the movement of the cart, she tried to order her thoughts. *No more tears.* She'd been plunged into this situation through no fault of her own and would need all her wits to survive. She'd hoped to dream of the goddess Mut and make a plea for help, but there'd been nothing but fragments of dreams and none had carried the ultra-clear feel of a vision or prophecy. Khian crossed her mind fleetingly, as she wished he was here as he'd been on the other occasions she'd been in jeopardy. Would he even think of her or wonder where she'd gone? Probably not, after all they'd only begun to circle each other in the timeless dance of a man and a woman. There'd been sweet promise implied, but no time to really explore what the potential between them was.

The cart jounced into a pothole, and she was thrown hard against the other side, banging her elbow. Biting her lip, she worked against the constriction of the chains to regain a seated position and soothed herself with a sip of lukewarm water. Once underway, a caravan never stopped, other than for an emergency like a sandstorm. It was going to be a long day.

She managed to create a small hole in the thatching of the wagon cover with her long fingernails, and peeked out periodically. Desert stretched as far as she could see, shimmering in the harsh sun. She could hear the sounds of animals, and men's voices cursing or yelling orders. Making the roll last as long as she could, nibbling tiny bites only every so often, she was nonetheless faint with hunger by the time the caravan stopped in the latter part of the afternoon.

Meketre untied the fabric and loomed into view, holding out his hand. "Come on, time to move into the tent for the night."

Awkwardly, she crept toward him and tried not to mind the touch of his hands as he lifted her out. He carried her toward a ring of tents set up around a fire.

"We're at an oasis," he said conversationally. "But there are none here who'd help a slave of mine so don't waste your breath calling out or making a fuss."

"If you want me to arrive at the ultimate destination in one piece," she said, deciding to push against his callous treatment of her," You need to put pillows into the wagon with me tomorrow. I'm bruised, and I almost broke my arm when the wheel went into a gully."

"Any other demands, great one?" he said.

"Apparently, I'm a commodity to you and even a lady of the court knows a thing of value sells better undamaged."

"You're in no position to bargain with me." He set her on the ground next to the tent pole and fastened her chains to the bronze loop. "Although I admire the effort. I'm not sure the sponsor of this effort cares overmuch what condition you're in, other than it must be alive and untouched by me or my men. But you are worth a great deal of gold." He raised a finger and glared at her as she opened her mouth to speak again. "Enough questions and cajolery. I'll have to gag you if you continue. Nothing you say is going to make any difference, and it's not my task to give you more information on your fate."

He left the area as Tentopet hurried in with a bowl of soup and more bread, which she set within Tuya's reach, silently as always. Glancing over her shoulder to be sure the master had left, she produced a wrinkled plum from the folds of her skirt and passed the fruit to Tuya. She squeezed the servant's hand in gratitude as she took the prize, receiving a shy smile in return, then Tuya was left alone with her thoughts.

Khian was hot, tired, and frustrated beyond belief. The day had been long and grueling, driving the caravan road. They'd come upon one long column of camels, donkeys and oxen fairly soon after leaving Thebes, and sought out the master. Nikare conducted a cursory conversation with the man off to the side as the caravan continued its progress west. Khian rested the horses, giving them water.

Shaking his head, the Medjai walked to the chariot and hopped up next to Khian. "Not one of the ones we're seeking. But I deemed it best to verify."

Silently, Khian steered the chariot into the road away from the caravan and urged the horses to a trot. 'Road' was putting too fine a point on it—this was a well-trodden path the caravans had been using for centuries, winding through the desert and passing oases large and small. The larger ones had small garrisons of Pharaoh's soldiers to keep order and fend off attacks from roving bands of nomads. They arrived at the first of these way station oases late in the afternoon as the sun was setting directly in front of them, and Khian took the chariot to the small set of buildings representing the official order. He identified himself, although the war chariot itself spoke of his rank, and gladly handed the horses over to the grooms, before he and Nikare went in search of the officer commanding the place.

The commander was happy to have official company and full of questions about events in Thebes and gossip at court, which Khian did his best to satisfy as he and his Medjai companion sat over a late dinner with the man and several of his senior sergeants. Khian noticed and admired how subtly Nikare wove his own questions in the conversation, learning as much as he could about the caravans camped within the safety of the oasis for the night, and which camel trains had passed through earlier.

As he and Nikare retired for the night to a suffocating, small vacant chamber in the officers' quarters, Khian said, "No sign of Tuya, or indeed anything unusual in the traffic."

"True, but I did verify the two caravans we seek have been and gone. Meketre's and Intef's both remain ahead of us."

The next day there were indeed pillows in the donkey cart when she was placed inside, as well as another full skin of water. Hastily, she made herself a nest of the pillows and gritted her teeth for another day of rough travel. Tuya let her thoughts roam to the large oasis of Kharga, which was the next major waystation on the caravan route. The city had a large contingent of Pharaoh's troops and a fort. She might even know a few of the officers, since this was a rotation post, and many might have been in Thebes prior to this assignment.

Racking her brain, she came up with a few names of men she believed were currently in the garrison. She had to get loose from the tent or the donkey cart, find an Egyptian soldier, and make a screaming scene until the officers would have to investigate. That was her plan.

She'd been examining the oddly decorated golden manacles and shackles constraining her movements, but the locks were intricate and she'd nothing to try picking them with. The butterfly and scorpion symbol made her uneasy if she stared at it for too long. There was something sly and off-putting about the juxtaposition of the beautiful airy creature and the deadly predator.

Her third night with the caravan passed in the same fashion as the previous two, with a long day of travel the next day. Through her hole in the thatch, she heard Meketre laughing and joking with Hewernef as they rode, both of them in an amazingly good mood.

The fourth night began the same as the others, with her meager dinner in the tent then lying down to sleep. After a few hours, Meketre and Hewernef came into the tent, the former shaking her awake, with his hand covering her mouth.

"We're going to meet your buyer now," he said.

"It's the middle of the night."

"An excellent time to leave the caravan with little fanfare." Meketre gagged her and flung a hooded cloak over her before carrying her out of the tent, his strong arms easily suppressing her attempts to struggle or cause delay. Although the hood was pulled low over her face, she could peek out from under the coarse fabric and see four camels waiting outside in the moonlight, three saddled and one with supplies.

Meketre slung her into one of the saddles, winding her chains around a convenient wooden, upward curving part of the saddle. She gasped behind the gag as the camel lumbered to its feet. She clung as tightly as she could to the saddle, afraid of falling.

Meketre hovered close until he was sure she had her balance. "We've a few days journey ahead of us. I'll take off the gag as soon as we're far enough away from the oasis."

Barely able to concentrate as her hopeful plans for getting help in Kharga were shattered, Tuya struggled to breathe, to think through this new development. Where could they be going? Would a nomad tribe have expended time and treasure to kidnap her? But who else could there be at an unknown destination in the desert?

Meketre and Hewernef mounted their camels and the small group set out into the desert, soon leaving the slumbering caravan far behind in the moonlight.

CHAPTER SIX

The two caravans in question had made good time on their westward trek. Khian and Nikare caught up to Intef's a day later. The caravan master wasn't thrilled to see them, but his demeanor was resigned and respectful. Intef certainly didn't act like a man with anything to hide. Khian was inclined to abandon this caravan and set his horses galloping after the other instead. Time to find Tuya was passing too fast. But Nikare was in charge of this aspect of their assignment and Khian had to tamp down his raging impatience.

"Must I stop my camels for your inspection, noble lords?" Intef asked with a touch of sarcasm as the stood next to the chariot, negotiating while the caravan itself continued on its slow way. "You do know it takes a long time to start up again, and my men and beasts will stand in the heat, waiting."

"We've no desire to be unreasonable," Nikare said smoothly. As agreed between them, Khian deferred to the Medjai. "We'll work our way down the line, interview a few of the drivers and passengers. Inspect some containers at random. We'll move as rapidly as possible. If we find nothing suspicious, we'll move on."

Intef nodded. "Very well then. Let's get this over with." He mounted his own camel and trotted to the head of the column to give the signal for an unscheduled stop.

Khian drove the chariot along the lengthy column at a walking pace. Nikare signaled him to stop periodically and would walk around a camel or donkey cart, examining the cargo panniers and engaging the driver in discussion. He also made a point of chatting with several groups of travelers, asking questions about the journey so far, and what they'd noticed about anyone joining or leaving the column.

After they'd reached the end of the caravan, and he'd questioned the final driver, Nikare hopped into the chariot and took a long drink from the waterskin. "You can give your horses their heads," he said. "Let's find Intef and tell him he can leave, then head for the next oasis ourselves."

"Nothing?" Khian lifted the reins, and the horses quickened their pace in response.

Nikare shook his head. "Nothing relevant to our search for the lady or to the tax inspectors we're supposed to be. Intef runs a clean operation apparently."

"I'm sure he'll be thrilled to hear the verdict, as we've held him hostage for hours on the road now."

The concept didn't appear to bother Nikare. "Cost of doing business in the Black Lands."

The caravan master glowered at them but wasted no time in getting his men up and running to set the column into motion. Nikare wrote a rapid note on a blank papyrus, handed it over, gave Intef an ironic salute then Khian was free to put his team into a gallop, venting his impatience in setting a dangerously fast pace. "What did you give him?"

"A certificate of inspection which he can use to avoid any further attention from Pharaoh's inspectors on the rest of the journey and the return. I made it broad." Nikare laughed. "Now he has a license to smuggle and convey illicit, unstamped goods, on this trip at least. He can recoup the lost profits from these hours."

Khian glanced over his shoulder at the caravan. "Do you think he will?"

With a shrug, the Medjai said, "I neither know nor care. It was a simple enough thing. Only one possibility left, my friend."

"Don't remind me. I hope we find this Meketre at the next waystation, and I pray to the gods Tuya is there as well."

"Fortunately, the place is large enough to have a garrison. We may need help, if we find her or indications she's hidden in the caravan's tents or crowd of passengers."

"I'll do whatever it takes to rescue her and commandeer the resources I need."

"I wish they gave me a military man as determined as you are on all of my cases," Nikare said. "You'd come in handy."

Khian's hopes were high and he was relieved to find the caravan they sought had indeed stopped at the next large oasis for the night. He and Nikare checked in with the local commander, handed his chariot horses over to the grooms and then were off to the site where the caravan in question had taken up temporary residence. Striding through the activity as the drivers unloaded cargo panniers and passengers set up their campsites, Khian said, "They must have recently arrived. It may be helpful to our search arriving while things are in disarray."

Their first setback came when they were directed to the caravan master by a sullen worker. "Meketre isn't in charge," the man said. He pointed to an individual shouting orders at several other men. "Thampthis runs the caravan this trip. Talk to him about whatever it is you need."

Surprised, Khian exchanged glances with Nikare then walked over to accost the master.

"We're seeking Meketre," Nikare said. "I'm Pharaoh's tax inspector and this is my partner, Captain Khian of Pharaoh's army."

Thampthis straightened and looked them both over from head to toe before spitting contemptuously in the opposite direction, as if he was one of his unruly camels. "What do you need him for?"

Nikare consulted a papyrus. "He's listed as master of this caravan. I need to conduct my inspection."

"Meketre isn't with us this trip. I'm the master. You need to inspect cargo now? While we're trying to unload and get set up for the night?"

"And where is Meketre?" Khian asked.

Thampthis glared at him. "He had other business. I'm not his keeper nor his master. He doesn't tell me what the specifics of his private trips are. Do you want to inspect my cargo or not?"

"Yes, we do. And question a sample of your passengers, as well." Nikare sounded almost apologetic. "Let me make a note about the change in master, and I'll be ready."

"As if the trip to Kharga wasn't challenging enough, now I have thrice damned inspectors underfoot. Meketre will owe me a bonus for this," Thampthis said. "This way then."

Khian admired the thorough manner in which Nikare went over the panniers containing various types of cargo and carts full of clay wine jars and interviewed passengers. He made a special effort to be friendly to several small children, asking them how the trip had been and working in his questions about anyone joining or leaving the caravan. Nikare asked to inspect a few tents, which seemed to astonish Thampthis but he agreed readily enough.

"You're nosier than any other inspector of Pharaoh's I ever had the misfortune to deal with," he said. "Are you new to this job?"

"Fairly new," Nikare said while Khian had to work hard to repress a laugh. "May we start with your tent?"

A servant girl was placing dinner on a low table inside the tent. She lowered her eyes and stood aside as Thampthis stood in the center of the carpet laid to cover the floor, threw out his arms and spoke loudly. "Here it is, my home on the road. Welcome to my humble abode. I regret I have nothing worthy of offering to two such distinguished officials of Pharaoh."

Khian noted the bulging wine sack the girl held, as well as the large and varied repast she'd been in the middle of setting out, but he said nothing.

Nikare did a rapid visual inspection of the tent. "We'll trouble you no further tonight, master Thampthis. Your cargo has been in order, save for the one shipment of wine sadly lacking stamps. I'm afraid we must confiscate the lot in its entirety and ship it to Thebes."

Thampthis swore a colorful oath and then said, "That merchant's barred from shipping anything with me again, I'll make sure he's banned."

"You'll deliver the wine to the garrison commander tonight?"

"Of course." The caravan master's agreement was grudging.

"Then we'll be on our way. You've been most accommodating." Nikare was smooth and gracious.

As they left the circle of campfires and camels, Khian opened his mouth to speak but Nikare shook his head slightly. Remaining silent until they'd entered the small fort, Khian said, "I saw nothing. I can't believe the goddess steered us wrongly, but if Tuya is here, she's well concealed."

"Don't give in to bitter despair yet. The servant girl wished to talk." Nikare grinned. "I think I'll sit beside the well for a while and listen to the musicians playing for spare deben from fellow travelers."

"You think she knows anything useful?"

Nodding, the Medjai said, "Oh yes. There's also this, Meketre was definitely in charge of the caravan when it left Thebes. So if this surly Thampthis is now the master, something happened along the road. I find the unexplained fact curious. What caravan master abandons his duty in the midst of the desert? And where would he go?" Nikare poured himself a beer and one for Khian. "I have no answers, mind you, but the fact questions exist is encouraging. There was also the issue of the tent pole."

Raising the mug to his lips, Khian paused. "I don't follow you."

"The tent pole had a sturdy bronze ring affixed to it, as if it'd been used to hold a prisoner. Unusual fixture for a caravan master's tent. We may yet learn more."

"I pray it be so," Khian said. "This was our last hope of finding Tuya. If I misinterpreted the birds as an omen, and she was taken in a different direction by one of the other caravans, she's lost." He had a pit in his gut no amount of beer would fill, an ache in the center of his heart. "Shall I join you at the well and appreciate the music?"

Nikare shook his head. "Better if I go alone. The girl was shy, uncertain. Two of us might intimidate her. If she comes to draw water, as I hope, I can set up a flirtation to cover a more serious conversation."

He didn't like it, but he recognized the wisdom of Nikare's approach, as well as the danger his own desperation to find Tuya might lead him to pressure the servant girl too much and never learn anything helpful. If indeed the woman knew anything useful. He headed to the stable to check the horses, mostly because he wasn't inclined to linger in the officers' mess and make conversation with the locals.

Later, Nikare found him there, the servant girl in tow. "Wise to come here," the Medjai said. "Private. This is Tentopet, and she has an interesting tale to share."

"The lady was kind to me," the woman said, eyes downcast. "She was sweet."

Khian took a deep breath to quell his excitement. "Lady?"

"Tell the officer what you shared with me," Khian said, moving to bar the stable door. "He's a friend of the lady."

"Really?" Tentopet turned to him with wide eyes and an awed expression. "And you came to rescue her? Like in a scribe's tale."

Khian was annoyed to have his private stake in the case put on display but, seeing how Tentopet reacted to the idea of a gallant rescue, he swallowed his embarrassed denial. "Indeed I've traveled like the wind to follow the trail. We may not have much time now."

She nodded. "We'd already left Thebes when Meketre caught up with us, bringing the beautiful lady bound and hidden in a basket. He chained her and kept her close in his tent."

Almost afraid to ask the question, Khian said, "Did he hurt her?"

Tentopet shook her head. "He told her whoever had paid for her wanted her alive and untouched. She did get badly bruised riding in the donkey, cart but she demanded pillows be provided."

"Good for her," Nikare said from the shadows by the door, approval in his voice for Tuya's spirit. "Tell him where Meketre went."

"Last night, he rose when the moon ascended into the sky. He and Hewernef took her into the desert. I—I was supposed to be asleep, but I wondered what was happening after I heard him giving Thampthis instructions for the remaining trek to Kharga. He told the lady there'd be several days of riding to reach her destination."

Grinding his teeth at being so close and missing Tuya and her captors by only a day, Khian said, "What direction did they go?"

"North, my lord, steering by the brightest star."

"But where were you camped at the time?" Nikare asked. "Not here."

"No, we took a detour from the main road a bit yesterday and stayed at a small oasis. There was no garrison there and no other caravan. Our passengers weren't pleased, or at least not those who travel the great road often." She frowned as if the complaints had been made to her personally.

"No one mentioned a detour when I questioned them today." Nikare's tone was slightly suspicious.

Her smile wide, the servant said, "Those who travel with us are not those who wish to assist a tax inspector."

"Fair enough." Khian rummaged in the chariot for the leather cylinder holding the maps then knelt, spreading the one for this part of the desert out on the floor. Cautiously, Nikare brought an oil lamp closer, to give better light. "We're here," Khian said, tapping one finger on a dot on the map. He scrutinized the papyrus for other dots and identified a faint one to the west of the great road, barely indicated by the mapmaker. "Might this be the other, smaller oasis?"

"The distance seems right," Nikare said. "What lies due north from there?"

Khian sat back on his heels. "Nothing."

"Meketre was confident," the girl said. "I think he'd been to this place before, on other trips. He sometimes disappears for a few days on the Kharga road."

"You've been extremely helpful," Nikare said. "Pharaoh will be grateful."

"I've been gone too long. I dare not rejoin my caravan," she said. "I've helped you—and the lady, who was so sweet—now you must help me."

"What is it you want?" The Medjai didn't display any surprise at her demand.

"There's a drover on a caravan going east. He and I—well, we've encountered each other at this oasis a few times in the past. He's said if I can escape my master, he'd marry me. His caravan is here now."

Khian exchanged looks with Nikare. "A thin reed to on which to place your hopes."

"Pinedjem is a good man. He's from the same province of Egypt where I grew up." Her protest was instant and hot. "He'd have paid my master the bride price long ago, but it's too high. Meketre has no desire to let me go, but Thampthis will only be annoyed and likely take no action."

"You need deben," Khian said. He rose and opened the leather pouch at his belt. "How much?"

She named a figure, and he doubled it, stating the bonus was given out of sheer gratitude that she'd taken the risk to give him news of Tuya. Her thanks were effusive as she hid the coins in a pouch of her own.

Nikare escorted her to the door. "Can you get safely to this Pinedjem? Do you want me to go with you?"

"Better if I go alone." She laid her hand on Khian's arm. "May the gods lead you to the lady."

"I'll tell her of your help," he promised. "Thank you."

Nikare opened the door a fraction and checked the surroundings. "All clear."

Without another word, she slipped past him and disappeared into the night.

"Good work," Khian said as Nikare joined him to stare again at the map. "I'm impressed. When can we leave?"

"I think in the pre-dawn light would be best, before Thampthis discovers her absence and comes to question us. Or worse, asks us to help find her."

"We could go now," Khian said, rolling the map carefully. As always impatience to be in motion, to take action to reach Tuya was foremost in his mind.

Nikare plucked a straw from a bale of dried grasses and chewed on it thoughtfully. "Are you moved by prophecy or a vision?"

"Neither, just impatience and worry for Tuya."

"It would be remarked as odd we left in the middle of the night. We can't slip away as quietly as a few camels on the fringe of the oasis." Nikare gestured as the stable around them. "We're in the middle of the encampment. Let us leave at the appointed hour I suggested, head west, and double back in a mile or so, once we locate this alternate track. I would expect Meketre is sleeping during the day, since he's traveling the desert. We can drive all day tomorrow, rest a few hours then drive at night ourselves. The moon will be bright and full for a few more days."

"The chariot goes well enough over the ordinary sands, but will flounder in deeper dunes," Khian pointed out. "We may be on foot soon."

Nikare stared beyond him, at the horses. "Or on their backs, riding as one does a camel. I've never seen it done, but it might be possible. But my hope is there's a track we can use. The girl said Meketre's gone on this odd side trip more than once, so perhaps the mysterious destination is reachable by road."

"There was none on the map."

"Many things exist that no scribe has drawn onto a piece of papyrus," Nikare said.

They followed the agreed upon plan and easily located the other oasis, which was occupied by a small family of nomads when Khian drove the chariot up to the edge of the sparse greenery. The leader of the group was soft spoken and showed no hostility, so Khian and Nikare made camp there for the night, each taking a shift remaining awake to guard the horses and the chariot.

"Keep your eyes open for anything resembling a road or a well-trodden path," Khian said after they'd progressed a few miles along a generally northern track. "The going is pretty rough at the moment. I'm not sure how long we can drive in this."

"We'll have to take shelter in the midday heat anyway." Nikare hopped down from the tail of the vehicle and jogged ahead of the horses. "We're lucky this is the travel season or we'd have to do this entire trip at night." He pointed to the left. "I think I see harder ground over there."

Khian drew the chariot to a halt while Nikare went to investigate.

The Medjai waved to him. "I think we've found a road."

"You're not serious? Who'd build a road out here?" He lifted the reins and clicked his tongue to get the horses to move in Nikare's direction.

Stamping his foot on the ground to demonstrate the hardness underneath, the police officer grinned. "Road."

Khian halted the team again and got down to investigate for himself, keeping tight hold on the reins. "By the jaws of Anubis, you're right. What's left of a road anyway. Must be centuries old." Shading his eyes with his hand, he surveyed the nearby terrain. "Hopefully, we can follow it for the most part. Who had the mad idea to build this and for what purpose?"

"Anyway, seems the men holding Tuya captive are taking her to this destination."

"Let's go." And Nikare was barely in the chariot again before Khian had flicked the reins to urge the horses onward again.

Khian was able to make better time as long as the road was available, and covered quite a few miles before the sun rose directly overhead. This forced them to shelter in a small wadi, where the naturally high stone walls of the canyon created shade. He and Nikare took turns dozing and, as soon as cooler breezes of late afternoon began, they hitched the horses to the chariot and set out once more. He drove past sunset and on into the night by the light of the moon, eventually halting to make camp and rest the horses.

Khian munched on dried meat and bread, washed down with warm beer. "I wish we'd seen vultures during the day. I worry we've gone astray."

"I understand your qualms, but the birds did send us on the right road originally. Maybe it's entirely up to us now." Nikare threw another dried dung patty on the fire and pivoted to listen as eerie howls split the night. "I'm no expert on desert travel, but I believed jackals hunted by day, alone or in mated pairs."

"As did I." The sound was eerie and bone chilling and coming from all directions. Khian got to his feet, hand on the hilt of his sword, the chariot at his back.

The horses moved restlessly on their tether line. Nikare came to stand beside Khian, shoulder to shoulder.

A breeze sprang up, unaccountably cold. The fire flickered and a cloud passed in front of the moon. The howling rose to a crescendo that hurt Khian's ears with its shrill notes and, as the moon again became visible, lighting the scene, he saw Anubis standing on the other side of the fire.

For a heartbeat only did he perceive the presence of the god then the vision was gone. "Did you see that?" he gasped, heart pounding.

Nikare nudged him in the ribs and pointed to the left with his knife.

Facing them was a warrior, easily seven feet tall, with straight black hair, strangely pointed ears like those of a jackal, two fangs protruding from his mouth in a canine fashion and glowing green eyes under a heavy brow accented by arched eyebrows. He wore a plain black kilt, held fast with a leather belt bearing the cartouche of Anubis as the buckle. He was barefoot. On his chest lay an elaborate pectoral collar of gold, jet, and turquoise. He had a sword and a belt knife, and carried a cowhide shield with the most detailed rendition of the god Anubis Khian had ever seen, drawn on the spotted gray and white surface in vivid colors. "The Lord of the Sacred Land has sent me to aid you." His voice was a low growl, as if a dog had been given language. "As he promised the World-Mother, I am to be a soldier under your command until the quest is completed." He saluted Khian.

Automatically, Khian returned the salute, swallowing hard. "Welcome to our fire. May we know your name?"

The uncanny soldier tilted his head, eyes gleaming with an inner light, again reminding Khian of a dog. "You may call me Ranefer."

The howling rose again, but thankfully sounded as if the jackals were moving away from his tiny campsite.

"I'm Khian, and this is Nikare. Would you like something to eat or drink?" He stumbled a bit over the normal courtesies to be accorded a fellow traveler.

Ranefer shook his head. "I've eaten." His impressive canine teeth flashed in the firelight. Now he came closer, and Khian had all he could do to stand his ground as the massive creature towered over him.

Ranefer lowered his head and sniffed. "You are distant kin."

"I'm from the Jackal Nome," he answered. "There are tales in the oldest family tombs hinting perhaps one of my ancestors bore a child to the Great One Anubis in human form, before even the time of the pyramid builders. I didn't believe them until now."

"The link is unmistakable to those with the Jackal's power." Seeming done with the subject, Ranefer said, "You should sleep while you can. I'll stand watch. We have much work ahead of us." He wheeled and strode to the other side of the fire, facing the desert. Raising his head, he gave a long howl, similar to the ones Khian had been hearing from the desert earlier. "Let those who roam the night be aware of my presence," said the uncanny soldier without turning to his companions. "Few there are who would wish to challenge me."

Nikare banked the fire. "Interesting family you have," he said in a low voice. "With resources like these why did you bother asking Pharaoh for help?"

"I didn't ask Anubis for help—the idea never would have occurred to me," Khian said as the other man sought his own sleep mat. "The goddess Mut made the request. Tuya is dear to her."

"I wonder if those who snatched her have any idea what they're up against?"

CHAPTER SEVEN

The second day of travel had gone much like the first, long hours of riding the swaying camel, Tuya clutching the saddle with her bound hands, and it continued well into the night. The dread in her heart deepened with each mile the small group covered, getting closer to her ultimate fate.

She glanced ahead in the moonlight and stiffened. Far ahead, a group of six figures stood in the middle of the desert. There were no beasts of burden nearby, no oasis, no structures of any kind. She blinked hard, unsure if one could see a mirage at night, but when she looked again, the eerie group was still there.

"Your welcoming committee." Meketre pointed with his coiled whip.

Mad thoughts of trying to stampede her camel, hopefully in another direction, ran through her mind, but Meketre had her animal on a tight lead. She couldn't fall from the saddle and hope to crack her skull on a rock either as he had her chains wound around the wooden protrusions of the frame. Terror grew in her heart the closer she rode to the waiting figures.

Finally, they were a few yards away, and Meketre gave the signal to halt. Other than the noises made by the complaining camels as the beasts knelt to allow their riders to dismount, the desert was quiet. Not even a breeze stirred the sand. Tuya was afraid to study the six people waiting too closely. The way the group stood silently watching was uncanny.

Meketre came to unhook her chains and lift her from the saddle. She fought the urge to cling to him. He might be her captor, surly and rough, but in that moment she desired nothing more than to ride away with him, rather than be handed over to the strange nomads.

Taking her by the hand, he dragged her forward. She took a deep breath and reached for her dignity as a lady of the court, straightening and doing her best to walk in the chains. She made herself look at the six people. In the center was a woman, whose face was obscured by the hood of her cloak, but the tight fit of her gown accented the curves of her body. On one side stood a man and on the other, slightly behind, was a servant, incongruously holding a tray with four mugs. It was the other three who terrified her the most. Tall and gangly, there was something not human about their stance, and their oddly shaped eyes glowed red. These guards carried spears and swords and stood poised as if to attack.

Meketre shoved her to her knees in front of the woman, holding her down with a hand on her shoulder as he talked. "I've brought exactly what you requested. She's young, of noble birth, educated, beautiful and highly placed, being a lady-in-waiting to the Royal Wife and counted as a friend of Pharaoh. Unmarried, no children, no family."

"Excellent." The woman's voice was melodic, almost hypnotic. She moved closer to Tuya, running her hand through her hair as one might do to a small child.

Tuya fought to control her trembling.

"But there's no need to be so rough with our new…guest." The woman made a tiny gesture. Meketre released his hold and stepped away. The woman raised Tuya to her feet, bracing her as she stumbled in the shackles, and the servant stepped forward, pausing beside Tuya. The leader of this odd group lifted a mug and put it into Tuya's hands, wrapping her cold fingers securely around the warmth of the cup. A delicious aroma wafted to her nose, rich spices and fruit. "The welcoming libation for a new arrival." Now the woman was handing Meketre a mug and beckoned for Hewernef to step forward and accept the third. She took the fourth and clinked it with Meketre's and the other man's. "To continued success," she said, drinking deeply.

Tuya had no desire to drink anything. She tried to pour the contents of her mug onto the sand. "I'm hardly going to accept the cup of a guest when I've been brought here in chains."

The servant grabbed her wrist with an unbreakable grip and prevented her from wasting the liquid.

"There'll be no need for chains or anger soon," said the woman, seeming undisturbed by Tuya's rudeness. "Much will be explained to you. I ask again—please drink deep."

Tuya had no choice because one of the giant guards came forward and held her head tilted with one clawed hand while he forced her mouth open with the other, despite her efforts to bite him. The servant poured the contents of the mug down her throat as if he'd done this act before. Gagging, she swallowed a great deal of the sweet potion and spit the rest out. There was an unpleasant metallic aftertaste. Almost immediately a warm lassitude swept through her limbs, and her head swam with dizziness.

"What poison have you given me?" she cried as the guard lowered her to the sands. She lay curled on her side, barely able to move.

"Merely a potion to calm your nerves and render you compliant," the woman said. She gestured to the man. "Bring forth the gold owed to the caravan master for his work on the commission I gave him."

Bowing, the other walked forward, one of the ominous guards at his back, holding a closed box. He stopped in front of Meketre, opening the lid to reveal the gleam of gold. Hewernef crowded his master, peering over his shoulder at the riches.

"Generous indeed," Meketre said. "The agreed upon amount and more. I hope we can do more business in the future, my lady."

"As to that, we shall see. There are others roaming the Black Lands at my command these days."

As if her words had been a signal, Meketre staggered, hand going to his throat. "I can't—I can't breathe." He clawed at Hewernef, who was now exhibiting signs of his own distress. Both men gagged and clawed at their clothing, trying to loosen their robes. First the master, then the drover fell to his knees then prone on the sand, making terrible noises, their bodies convulsing in pain.

Tuya closed her eyes against the gruesome sight. She struggled against the all-encompassing lassitude in order to speak. "Am I to die in the same manner?"

Her new captor laughed. "Oh no, there are far grander things in store for you. I had wine, you had the goddess's tea made from the palest of night blooming purple flowers, and the men had venom of the scorpion, distilled with other ingredients. Fortunately, I didn't mix up the mugs." She winked as if they were co-conspirators.

The added cruelty of letting Meketre touch his golden reward before he died wasn't lost on Tuya. She was in the grip of truly frightening people, and she shuddered to think what fate might be awaiting her. She was having a hard time remaining conscious as the drug she'd been given in the drink coursed through her body.

"Come," said the woman. "Time to return to the city."

She raised both hands to the sky and chanted in a language unfamiliar to Tuya. Even as drugged as she was, she felt a tingle as whatever magic the woman called upon began to work. One of the gray cloaked guards plucked her from the sands and held her effortlessly.

Tuya averted her eyes from his inhuman gray face and eerily glowing red eyes. The sand begin to swirl in front of her, glinting gold and bronze as a dust devil grew from the sky to the ground in an instant, lightning bolts striking the desert within the cylinder of rotating sands. A boom of thunder sounded loud enough to physically buffet Tuya's body, and a cavern opened in the sands. Lights flickered on garishly colored wall paintings and a flight of stairs led into the depths of the earth.

"You dwell in the underworld?" she asked, not sure she was speaking aloud.

Again the woman found her remark amusing, laughing. "Wait and see. You'll sleep soon and awaken in my wondrous home, the hidden city of Isidu-Ur."

As the group moved toward the gaping opening, Tuya found she couldn't keep her eyes open. The guard holding her passed under the arch of the tunnel or cave, and she gave up the struggle, allowing herself to drift into darkness, with a whispered prayer to Mut to deliver her from the nightmare.

As Khian drove the chariot ever north the next night, Ranefer easily jogging beside the horses, odd lightning streaked the dark skies ahead and he heard one boom of thunder.

"Strange time for a storm," Nikare said, tightening his grip on the chariot rail.

"Not a storm." Ranefer sounded positive.

What then? Khian decided not to ask the question, fearing he wouldn't like the answer, but kept the horses moving at a steady pace. Here the old road seemed practically untouched, which made the driving easier.

A few miles back he'd even seen the remnants of a line of statues, which must have once been truly magnificent, rivalling those of the Pharaohs'. Only the plinths were left of most, but one had a body resembling a lion, now headless, and in another spot they'd passed a single giant stone wing, lying half buried.

"Who lived here?" Nikare had asked. "I thought this had always been barren desert, empty save for a few hardy nomad tribes."

"Old civilizations now lost in time," Ranefer answered, turning his head for a moment. "As to the issue of where the desert encroaches, there's history beyond the reach of your knowing. The gods keep records in the library of Thoth."

"You've read these records?" Khian was amazed that the soldier, who he believed was an actual jackal molded into human shape by the god, would have spent time in such an activity.

Ranefer gave a laugh sounding curiously like a jackal's bark. "Not I, captain. But the Lord of the Sacred Land has imparted certain knowledge to me to aid in our quest."

"I see something or someone, lying on the sands," Nikare said, pointing.

Khian saw the bundles of rags as well and encouraged the horses into a gallop with voice and whip. They arrived at the spot a few moments later, and Nikare jumped from the chariot to run to the bodies. Khian joined him, holding the reins.

"I'm guessing this is the missing Hewernef and master Meketre," Nikare said, pointing at the tattoo on one corpse's wrist.

"Died a pretty awful death, from the condition of the bodies." Khian examined the ground. "Quite a few tracks here—we didn't miss whoever it was that killed them by much." He clenched his fists in frustration, to have been so close to Tuya again. "No sign of Tuya. Whoever killed them and stole their camels must have taken her. But was this the group she was kidnapped for?"

"I would guess the answer is yes. Bloody as these two are, they have no wounds. If bandits or hostile nomads ambushed them, there'd be signs of a fight. Perhaps the one who set this entire plot in motion felt the henchmen had outlived their usefulness, much as Anen did, in Thebes." Nikare rendered his professional opinion dispassionately.

"Ruthless." Khian fought a ripple of despair over Tuya's fate.

Nikare rose to walk carefully on the sands, where the night breeze was already moving the grains to obliterate the marks. "Four camels." He pointed. "By the tracks and dung."

Khian frowned. "Your tally can't be right. Whoever Meketre met here would have had their own camels or a cart. If these ominous new players were on foot, they'd still be in sight." He gestured toward the horizon. "Nothing."

"The footprints are strange," the Medjai said. "I'd say two women, so possibly one was Tuya, and a couple of men. But then there are clawed prints like nothing I've ever seen."

"Rabisu." Ranefer had stood silent while the two men examined the scene. "Demons of olden times, not of the Black Lands." He bared his fangs. "I smell the stench."

Nikare walked in an ever widening circle, eyes fixed on the ground. "No signs of anyone leaving this spot."

"So where did they go?" Khian was uneasy.

Ranefer pointed at the ground. "The scent lies there."

Khian stared at the point he indicated then back at the jackal warrior. "I don't understand."

"Magic?" Nikare asked. "How can we follow them then?"

"Has she been taken into the underworld?" Khian asked. "I'll follow her wherever the trail leads, even into the Lake of Fire if I must, but how do we gain access?"

Ranefer knelt beside the spot he'd indicated. Laying his shield carefully on the sands, with the image of Anubis face down, he said, "The Lord of the Sacred Land owns this desert of the west." Raising his face to the night sky, he howled. The sound was eerie and powerful. Echoes came from all directions as actual jackals picked up his cry and passed it onward.

Khian felt goosebumps all over his body, and the hair rose on the back of his neck as the sound continued. Clouds gathered directly overhead and the moon's light dimmed. With a loud crack, a bolt of red lightning spiraled down from the clouds and struck the shield, which glowed as if on fire. Lines of ruby red ran from the shield in all directions, and the sand retreated from the light. Ranefer stopped vocalizing, snatched his shield from the ground, and retreated. Khian and Nikare moved in unison with him.

A yawning pit opened in the earth, and Khian glimpsed stairs leading into the depths.

"We must go," Ranefer said. "The door won't be open for long."

"The horses—I can't leave them here to die if we don't make it," Khian said. "Help me get them free of the chariot." He ran to the team, loosening the buckles and straps as Nikare came to assist. With flapping arms the men drove the horses further from the chariot until the frightened animals kicked up their hooves and galloped away. Grabbing the bow and a quiver of arrows from the chariot to add to his armament, Khian sprinted to where Ranefer waited on the top step, Nikare at his heels.

The men descended the stairs as thunder rumbled in the sky behind them. Sand rained down on their heads as the mouth of the cavern closed behind them.

The walls were painted with elaborate depictions of gods and people unfamiliar to Khian, not at all in the Egyptian style. The paint was vivid, and several of the pigments glowed in the dark, providing enough light for him to see the tunnel ahead. Winged lions covered the walls, reminding him of the abandoned, ruined statues he'd driven past on their way to this spot. Inscriptions in a peculiar wedge-shaped form ran along the border of the cave wall, as if explaining the paintings.

Khian traced his hand along the wall where their entrance had been. Only solid stone remained. "I hope you can work a similar spell to get out when it's time to leave," he said to Ranefer.

The warrior shrugged, drawing his sword. "It will be as the Great One Anubis wills. I smell the rabisu strongly here—let us follow the trail."

"Personally, I'm more worried about explaining to Edekh why I lost one of Pharaoh's chariots and the horses," Nikare joked as he stepped from the last stair onto the flat surface of the tunnel.

As they proceeded, there were several times another tunnel branched off from the main route, but each time Ranefer strode a few feet into the side passageway and shook his head emphatically. "Not where we need to go."

Khian walked with his two companions for perhaps half an hour, when he saw faint light ahead, which grew brighter as he drew closer. The tunnel ended on a ledge, and Khian realized he was at a vantage point overlooking a good sized city, located in a bowl shaped valley, open to the night sky but completely surrounded by steep rock walls. A small river ran through the valley, emerging from the eastern rock face and disappearing into a cavern in the cliffs on the western side.

The moonlight was strong enough to make the details fairly clear. At first he thought the city was asleep, but then as he continued to evaluate the situation, he decided it was partially abandoned. The houses and other buildings closest to the cliff where he stood were in poor condition, with cracked and fallen walls, and roofs with holes or collapsed entirely. Toward the center of the city fires and lamps glowed, so at least there were some occupants remaining.

At the actual city center lay a small, terraced plateau, upon which stood a complex of structures reminding him of a palace or a temple, or perhaps both. Lights blazed there, and he could see the figures of guards walking the edges of the topmost terraces. None of the architecture was in the Egyptian style of building.

"What is this place?" Nikare asked Ranefer.

"Does it matter?" Khian asked. "We have to find Tuya and get out. I'm guessing she'll be held captive there." He pointed with his chin at the central plateau. "Now, how do we get down from here and into the city?"

"Steps over here," Ranefer said, moving to the right side of the ledge.

The stairs he'd found were ancient, slippery with moisture and moss, but Khian and his companions managed the descent in fairly short time. Standing on a broad road that appeared to be in fair condition, he said, "The people we're following didn't bring camels down the path we just took."

"Perhaps the animals were taken into one of the other tunnels we saw." Nikare looked at the sky. "It's going to be daylight soon. Do we have a plan?"

"Infiltrate the city and observe from hiding for now," Khian said, relieved to be setting strategy. "When night falls again, we'll work our way into that big building on the hill. These people are overconfident of their security, not posting even one guard here at the tunnel. Let's hope their vigilance is similarly lax elsewhere." He moved to take the lead and headed toward the nearest house, taking cover in the shadows as the other two followed him.

They'd moved closer to the occupied center of the city when Ranefer paused, sniffing the air. "The rabuisu hunt."

"Us?" Khian asked.

The jackal soldier bobbed his head in agreement.

"Get inside, quick." Khian tugged on Nikare's arm. "These houses are a maze, all connected. We can hide."

Khian ran ahead of the other two to the nearest door and slid inside, sword at the ready, moving aside for Ranefer and Nikare to pass. The house they were in had no roof in places, so although the visibility was poor it was enough for them to move upstairs into the second floor. From there they hurried onto the roof, where Khian went to the low parapet and peered over. A hooded figure prowled the street where they'd been.

The creature glanced up, eyes glowing red. Khian shrank back, unsure if the demon had seen him. "Move," he whispered, gesturing with his sword. "To the next roof."

The houses were packed together, and he led his companions across three roofs in quick succession before descending a broken flight of stairs. He ran through the destroyed house and out the gaping hole in the rear kitchen area. Nikare and Ranefer jogged on his heels, and Khian worked his way through an overgrown grove of stunted fruit trees before he took shelter inside the gaping door of another structure. "Is he still on our trail?"

Fangs exposed, Ranefer tested the air. "He might have lost the scent."

"Good." Khian leaned against the wall and took a deep breath. "Maybe we've found our den for the day."

"The sun is rising," Nikare said.

Khian peered outside. "Seems we've stumbled into someone's garden." The large area behind the houses was a well-tended plot of ordered rows of greenery he recognized – onions, leeks, cabbage, radishes, and more.

"For sure no one lives in this tumbled down wreck," Nikare said.

"Maybe the owner comes from the center of the city to garden."

Ranefer made a silencing motion. "The demon passes."

Khian pressed his back to the wall and kept as quiet as he could.

A woman's voice broke the quiet. She was singing what he recognized as an old song, coming closer. Cautiously, he peered past the crumbled edge of the broken door. The newcomer set a basket on the ground as he watched and began harvesting ripe cabbage from the edge of her garden.

Ranefer voiced a low growl and launched himself out the door. A gray-cloaked rabisu broke through a brick wall as if it were papyrus and sprinted toward the woman, taloned hands extended. She screamed and tried to rise but tripped over the hem of her dress and fell.

"Set's teeth." Khian swore and ran to assist Ranefer. "Get the girl to safety," he yelled to Nikare.

The jackal warrior made an inhuman leap and collided with the rabisu in midair, both combatants slashing with fangs and claws, falling to the ground in a tangle of growling, kicking bodies. Khian hovered for a moment, sword at the ready, then cursed as he sheathed the blade and grabbed the bow he had slung across his back. Notching an arrow, he waited for the right moment, prayed to Anubis, and released the shaft with deadly aim. The bronze tipped arrow struck the demon in the arm and hardly slowed it down at all. The beast simply yanked the arrow free with a snarl.

The movement gave Ranefer an opening, however, and he went straight for the throat, sinking his fangs deep into the demon, heedless of the glowing red ichor spraying from the wound.

Khian slung his bow and grabbed his sword once more, wading in to slash at the creature's legs. The demon couldn't fight both of them effectively and collapsed to the ground, where Ranefer fell upon it, tearing at the flesh until the other stopped moving. Extending his claws, the jackal ripped into the chest cavity and yanked out a mass of oozing black flesh, not recognizable as a heart—although Khian thought surely that's what the organ was. Ranefer devoured the morsel in three bites.

Khian stepped forward to touch his arm. The supernatural warrior wheeled in a threatening manner, taloned hands raised in a defensive posture, but the light of combat in his eyes faded as he focused on Khian.

Khian eyed the jackal. "Did he inflict serious damage upon you?"

"Bah, I heal in an instant. His ilk can't destroy a warrior of Anubis." Ranefer stood tall. "This demon was old, but not as powerful as his kind are said to be. Living in this city has weakened him."

"I hope the others will be similarly vulnerable." Khian sheathed his sword. "We need to hide the body."

"The putrid corpse hides itself." Ranefer pointed, and Khian watched the demon dissolve in a stomach-turning fashion, as if melting from the inside out. The ground soaked up the fluids and soon there'd be no sign of the rabisu other than an area of dead vegetation.

"Good." Khian swung around to see what was happening with Nikare and the woman they'd rescued.

She was leaning hard on the Medjai. "My family has farmed this plot since we arrived," she said in a trembling voice. "The demons never bothered us before."

"He was after us," Khian said, moving to her side. "I'm sorry you caught his attention."

"Are you from the Black Lands? Egyptians?" she asked, glancing from Nikare to Khian.

He found her question odd since she was apparently Egyptian herself. "Yes, but we can't stand here talking. We should find another hiding place before we attract any more attention, demonic or otherwise. I'm sorry, but you'll have to come with us for now. I can't risk you reporting our presence to whoever is the authority here."

"Queen Ninkurra Azimua of the Halaqu rules here, with the help of the demons, as you saw." The woman's voice was disdainful as she intoned the ruler's name. Apparently she wasn't a devoted subject. "We can go to my house on the far fringe of the living city. I dwell alone, and if we go now, before full light, none will remark upon you."

"Lead the way." Khian decided to trust her up to a point. He drew his belt knife and held it to her throat, ignoring the startled glance he got from Nikare. "I warn you I'll kill you myself if you betray us."

The woman seemed unfazed by his blade, tossing her hair. "I'm Merneith of the Caravan People, and my loyalty lies with the Pharaoh of Egypt, if there still is one. I'll gladly help you with whatever brings you here."

"If there still—" Khian swallowed the rest of his amazed exclamation over her statement. "We serve the Great One Nat-re-Akhte who wears the two crowns and rules all of Egypt."

"Too much talk," Ranefer said, the growl in his tone again. "I scent no enmity or betrayal in her. Let us go."

Merneith led them along a narrow path winding among the old houses. Gradually the neighborhood became less dilapidated, although apparently uninhabited. The structures were in better repair than those on the perimeter Merneith stopped at a large, two story building showing faded traces of blue and red paint. "This is my home. I welcome you to my house in peace."

She made to step inside, but Khian held her arm and preceded her, sword at the ready. The first floor was one open space with sparse furniture, but he noted several musical instruments, including a large harp. He took the stairs to the second floor and checked those rooms quickly. "All clear."

Apparently not offended by his suspicions, Merneith went to the cooking area. "Are you hungry? May I offer you anything?"

"Very gracious of you, my lady," Nikare said. "I'm parched and emptiness makes my gut rumble."

"I breakfasted well," Ranefer said with a snap of his jaws.

Remembering the meal the jackal soldier had made of the rabisu's heart, Khian repressed a shudder. "We don't want to be a burden on your resources," he told their hostess.

"No burden. I don't have anything fancy to offer – fruit and bread, with beer." She was busy filling a communal plate. "Make yourselves comfortable."

"I'll stand watch from the roof." Ranefer moved to the stairs.

Nikare and Khian sat on the chairs Merneith indicated, and she deposited the tray on a small table between them, returning to her kitchen for the promised beer.

"Do you play?" Khian gestured at the harp.

"Yes, I live out here away from the rest because I like to practice and to write new songs at all hours." As she handed him a mug full of beer, she grinned. "Not all neighbors appreciate hearing unfinished songs over and over while the artist creates. And there are plenty of houses to pick from, as I imagine you saw for yourself." She retrieve a plate and mug for herself then rejoined them. "What brings you to the hidden city of Isidu-Ur?"

"Someone here seems to have arranged for the kidnapping of a highborn lady," Khian said, deciding to keep Tuya's true status as a member of the royal court to himself for the moment. "We were sent to rescue her."

"What is this place? It's not on any maps of the area," Nikare asked. "How came you to be here?"

"As to the city, I can only tell you what the Isidu-Ur elite people say of themselves. Many centuries ago, long before the pyramid builders, they were a vast power, aided by armies of rabisu. Yet they had enemies, who worshipped other gods and were served by their own demon armies. In a terrible assault on all their cities, the Halaqu people went down in defeat. The enemy was merciless, determined to wipe the empire from the face of the world."

"I'd say their opponents succeeded since I never heard any of this history before." Khian vowed to ask Ranefer if the Library of Thoth contained anything about this.

"Or of those who conquered," Nikare added.

Merneith shrugged. "I can only repeat what I was taught as a child. The woman who is queen was a much beloved daughter of the king at the time, and a priestess of the goddess Inanna. The goddess felt much loyalty and love for Ninkurra and was sympathetic to her pleas not to be taken by the enemy. Inanna granted her a set of demon bodyguards and allowed her as well to take a large number of her courtiers with their households to flee the slaughter. The group ran to this secret city, which was originally built by the king as a private garden spot. The goddess gave Ninkurra special power to keep herself and the city safe, and so they've lived here in isolation for all the centuries since their own kingdom crumbled to dust. I was told the word Halaqu in their language means something to the effect of 'the disappeared'."

"You spin a scribe's tale of magic. Are you then a storyteller as well as a musician?" Despite having seen magic in action himself since Tuya had been kidnapped, the story she was reciting seemed utterly fantastical.

"As to the truth of my story, you encountered the rabisu. If you're unfortunate enough to meet the queen, you'll believe me. According to the elders, she's been unchanging since my people were taken over two hundred years ago. So I can easily believe she's been here for centuries longer." Merneith made a sweeping gesture. "Just look at the city around us, with so much fallen to wrack and ruin. At one time there was quite a population."

Nikare leaned closer. "That's the third time you've referenced your people being taken. How did a group of Egyptians come to dwell in this place, among the others?"

She refilled her beer mug and offered the pitcher to him. "Two hundred years ago a large caravan became hopelessly lost in a sudden sandstorm, caught out in the open desert with no shelter. Many died. The survivors were rescued by the residents of Isidu-Ur and brought to the hidden city to rest and recuperate. Or so they thought. When the group tried to leave, the queen informed them they were her new citizens, sent by the goddess to replenish the diminishing population of her city. None could leave. A group of men made an attempt and were slaughtered by the rabisu, including my grandfather, leaving his pregnant wife a widow. After the killings the survivors were given their choice of the empty houses and told to forge themselves into a village. To work."

"As slaves?" Khian said.

"For the common good. For the most part, the elite don't interfere with us. We have our own council of elders, and as a village we do tithe to the queen--"

"But you can't decide to leave." He interrupted. "Slaves in effect even if self-governing."

Merneith nodded. "After the first rebellion, people gradually grew accustomed to the way things were. The second generation knew no other way of life, and now most of those who were born into the third generation, like me, can't imagine another. Egypt is a legend, as lost to us as their home is to the Halaqu. The youngest of our people, the children, don't even speak of it."

"And do you accept this state of affairs so easily?" Nikare asked.

She shook her head and rose to walk to the harp, strumming her fingers across the strings to bring forth a melancholy chord. "I long to see the world, to break free, and play my music. To travel away from here and never return. Truth be told, that's part of why I live here, outside the village. The elders think I'm a bad influence, although the queen requires me to teach my musical skills to several of the children, so the skill remains alive for her pleasure." Merneith played a snippet of another song before pivoting on her heel. "If I help you find this kidnapped lady, will you take me with you when you leave?"

Before Khian could open his mouth to say yea or nay, Nikare had risen and walked to her, resting one hand on her shoulder. "We'll do all in our power, my lady. But we're on a dangerous mission and leaving this place may not be easy."

She stared into his eyes for a moment before flicking her gaze to Khian.

"Since my friend has given his word, I'll honor it," he said with reluctance for complicating the mission by adding another person to be taken to safety. If Merneith was able to assist them she'd certainly earn her passage and right of protection. "But first we have to find Lady Tuya."

"If the queen had her kidnapped, she'll be in the palace. I've been summoned tonight along with the other musicians and the village dancers, to provide entertainment at a special dinner." Merneith folded her arms. "I'll see what I can find out."

"Can you provide us with the layout of the palace interior?" Khian asked.

"Only a few places. We villagers aren't allowed into most of it and never into the temple. I've been to the queen's chambers once or twice." She strummed a light tune. "She wished for music to lighten her mood."

"It's more information than we had before," Khian said. "Anything will help."

"But why are you so sure the lady you seek is hidden in Isidu-Ur?" Merneith collected the remnants of their breakfast and stepped into her cooking niche.

Nikare brought the beer mugs to her and lingered beside her in the niche. "We saw the bodies of the known kidnappers, Meketre and Hewernef on the sands, close to where the entrance for the city lies."

Reaching for the mugs, at the names of the kidnappers she startled and one mug crashed to the floor, breaking into fragments.

Nikare set the other two on a table and caught her hands. "You knew them?"

"Meketre was the name of the master of the original caravan, the one my grandparents were with. He made a deal with the queen that he and a few of his men could leave the city, in exchange for serving as her eyes and ears to the outer world, and for bringing her whatever she requested. He took an oath in her temple and was marked with the butterfly and scorpion. Meketre is a hated name, an object of scorn, for leaving all the others trapped in the city. I had no idea his descendants still honored the bargain with her."

Khian and Nikare quizzed her about a few other details of the city and how it was guarded, but then she insisted she had to practice for the evening's concert. Khian drew the Medjai outside as the beautiful music poured from the harp.

"Unwise to make promises to the woman," Khian murmured. "Even if we survive this mission and get Tuya to freedom, Merneith will be a lost lamb in Egypt. Any knowledge she has is two centuries out of date. How will she make her way?"

"If we rescue Tuya and return to Pharaoh's court, the queen will be more than happy to add one musician to her retainers, I'm sure. Especially if Merneith helps us. We can keep her secrets."

Khian didn't feel as sure, but Nikare's knowledge of Thebes and the royal court was more than he'd ever know, so he deferred to the Medjai. "Certainly having an ally who can get into the palace here is useful."

"Your face shows doubt," Nikare said. "You don't trust her?"

"Do you? She could be lying to us to save herself. At any rate, we won't be waiting here for her. We'll withdraw into the ruined quarter again, and I'll meet her alone at an appointed hour while you and Ranefer stand watch from a distance."

"Good precautions." Nikare nodded toward the house, where music still played. "I'd hate to think one who can create such enchantment for the ears and who longs for freedom could betray us."

"And you're the police officer." Khian clapped his friend on the shoulder. "You should be more skeptical than I. Perhaps her beauty and demeanor are penetrating the shield of your good sense."

Nikare snorted. "Maybe. I'll admit I find her attractive."

"And for that reason, I'll go give her my instructions for meeting this evening, after the banquet, while you stand guard."

CHAPTER EIGHT

Tuya awakened slowly, as if surfacing from under the waters of the Nile, her mind fuzzy and slow. She blinked and stretched, trying to pull strength into her limbs. Remembering the last few moments before the rabisu had carried her away, she sat up in the bed and examined her surroundings.

She was no longer wearing the bedraggled maid's garb, but had clearly been bathed and dressed in a filmy white shift, tied at the shoulders with broad red ribbons. Tuya felt nauseous at the idea of unknown persons touching her while she'd been unconscious, but what was done was done. Her greatest concern now was to figure out where she was and how to escape. She swallowed hard, filled with dread that escape would be as impossible as fleeing from the caravan had been.

The room was bright and sunny, with colorful wall paintings in a style unknown to her, using colors and symbols whose hard edges and shapes were jarring to her eyes. Beside the bed, there was a table, a chair, and several covered baskets.

What caught her eye and brought her stumbling from the bed was a set of shelves built into the wall, where a myriad of items sat. Tuya touched rings, earrings, bracelets, fancy sandals, folded pieces of fabric that might have been dresses at one time, all displayed as if laid out by a merchant for a high born lady to make her selections. Most were gold, encrusted with precious stones and enamel inlays. A few were set with pearls. Tuya touched a pair of hair combs in the shape of lotus flowers then picked up a ring sitting next to them on the shelf. She flipped the ring in her fingers and saw a tiny inscription inside the band, a cartouche, but the name was meaningless to her.

A door stood next to the wall with the shelves, and she went through it quickly, hoping for a way out. She found herself on a balcony, but the wall was high. Complicated scrollwork rose above the stones, which was meant to prevent her from throwing herself off, she guessed. Peering through the slats, Tuya observed a compact city laid out far below, with a small river cutting through the center, the whole surrounded by sheer stone walls. Above lay only the pure blue of the sky.

Tears in her eyes, she stood with her hands clenched on the lattice and made a silent vow. Whatever purpose she'd been brought here to fulfill, she'd do her best to resist. To escape. To thwart her captors. *Help me, Great One, please. I just want to get home.*

She thought she heard a sound high in the sky and impatiently brushed the salty tears from her eyes to squint at the brilliant morning. Were those vultures flying over the city? Or merely her own desperate wish for the goddess to hear her?

The sound of the door opening made her spin on her heel, stepping back into the bedroom.

"I'm so glad to see you up and about." A woman had entered, moving swiftly to the chair and seating herself as if on a throne. She wore garish clothes marking her immediately as a foreigner to Egypt. Her dress was a deceptively simple sheath, save for a border of red overlapping, feather-shaped panels, in three tiers, sweeping the floor. Over one shoulder the woman wore a draped panel of sheer fabric, painted with red flowers. Her ebony black hair was elaborately dressed, accented with golden pins. Enormous red coral and gold earrings dangled from her ears. Her face seemed young but upon closer examination, there were lines and a few white hairs threaded their way among the glossy black strands.

Tuya had never seen anything remotely like the woman's outfit, and she'd attended many functions with foreign dignitaries in Pharaoh's court before. Tuya had no idea what land this woman was from. *And no idea, therefore, where I'm being held captive.* Her stomach sank with despair.

The woman gave her a small smile, mock conciliatory. "No aftereffects from the drugged drink, I hope?"

"You can't keep me here," Tuya said.

Laughing, her enemy said "On the contrary, I can do anything I like in my own city. But please, let's not have hostile words to mar the purity of the morning. You're my guest--"

"Then let me leave." Tuya stood with her fists clenched. The gray-skinned demon standing beside the door watched her closely, and she knew she'd never even get close to the woman seated in the chair if she followed her instinct to attack.

A tiny frown appeared, a furrow in the woman's brow, almost imperceptible under her elaborate—and to Tuya's eyes, gaudy – makeup. "Don't waste my time." Drumming her fingers on the chair's arm, she smiled again. "As I was saying, you're my honored guest until the time arrives for the ceremony of renewal. We should introduce ourselves, by the way. I'm Ninkurra Azimua, queen of the city. And you are?"

"Tuya, senior lady-in-waiting to Ashayet, Royal Wife of Pharaoh Nat-re-Akhte."

"Hmm, not the same man wearing the double crowns as the last time I had a guest—I can't wait to hear all about him and the state of the world now." She gestured at the wall. "Pity you didn't bring anything to add to my collection. Meketre was supposed to acquire something of your personal effects, for me to remember you by when our time has ended, but he failed in that simple task. He was often incompetent, unlike his father and grandfather. Fortunate for me I have a few other agents to call upon outside the valley."

Tuya swung around to stare at the shelves of treasure. "You kidnapped all these women?"

"Most were residents of my city, my subjects. A few I acquired from the outer world, high born women brought here on my orders, yes." Ninkurra nodded. "And each lived here as my guest, treated to every luxury my staff can provide until their moment of service arrived." She rose, smoothing the fabric of her gown. With one small gesture, she summoned several maids who'd evidently been waiting in the hallway. The servant's dresses were simpler versions of the same design the queen wore. Further proof Tuya was in unknown territory now.

"Enjoy your breakfast." The queen moved toward the doorway out.

Tuya took an involuntary step to follow her. "Wait—what's going to happen to me? Why have you brought me here?"

Ninkurra shook her head. "We'll talk again later."

The two maids hastened to leave, and the rabisu guard shut the door with a slam as he too departed.

Hunger was the last thing on her mind, but Tuya approached the repast spread on the table anyway, figuring she'd better try to keep her strength up. She eyed the food and drink with suspicion, remembering the drugged cup the queen had given her out on the sand. Accordingly Tuya tried to choose items that were hardest to tamper with. There were no utensils, not even a spoon. Defiantly she took her selections onto the balcony and ate there, hoping for another glimpse of the vultures.

She was left alone all day and made a noon meal of the leftover fruits and bread. She spent most of her time on the balcony, where there was an illusion of freedom. Tuya tried breaking a plate and using the sharp fragments to dig at the latticework, which proved a frustrating task, yielding not much result. She tried the door but found it was securely locked on the outside. The baskets held nothing useful as far as making an escape.

She stared at the finery left behind by those who'd been prisoners in this room before. 'Moment of service' sounded ominous, and clearly these women had never needed their clothing or jewelry again. Rubbing her arms, Tuya shivered. The queen had been so calm and matter of fact. How many people had she killed?

As the shadows grew longer in the late afternoon, her dark and racing thoughts were interrupted by the arrival of the maids. Two women removed the dishes and the remnants of the food, even going outside to clean the balcony.

Apparently, she wasn't the only captive who'd sought refuge on that lonely, cramped space above the city. A third maid brought in another gown, less sheer, decorated with the petal-shaped ruffles and drapery much like the queen's dress had featured. A fourth woman stood by the door, hands clasped on her stomach.

"You're Egyptian," Tuya said with relief. "Please tell me what's going on here."

"I'm your translator," she said. "Few of the Isidu-Ur have bothered to learn Egyptian, unlike the queen. All the ceremonies tonight will be in the pure language of the city people, and her majesty wishes you to understand what is said."

Tuya's mind was full of questions, like a net full of slippery fish, but she took a deep breath and forced herself to smile. "I'm Tuya, and you are?"

"Sidjehuti."

"What kind of ceremony will I be facing tonight? Is this what the queen referred to as my 'moment of service'?" *And please let it not be that.*

"I'm not here to answer your questions, merely to translate what is said to you by others. The queen will tell you what she wishes you to know." Sidjehuti's voice was prim, and she seemed nervous, glancing at the maids, who were watching them with narrowed eyes. After a moment she unbent a little. "The queen will give you proper instructions to perform the service, but the sacred ceremony is not tonight. This evening is a banquet to allow her court to see you and judge your worthiness."

The maids seemed impatient and closed in on Tuya, trying to unfasten the red ribbons holding her dress. The women spoke harshly in a guttural language that sounded like gibberish to her. Hands raised, she backed away. "What do they want?"

"The maids are here to assist you in dressing, do your hair and makeup, and ensure you present the best aspect possible to the court." Sidjehuti looked her up and down. "They say the clothes you wore upon your arrival didn't fit the claim you make of nobility. The offending and coarse garments have been burned."

"I don't have to explain myself to them or to you." Tuya was annoyed at herself feeling defensive over the criticism. She'd been masquerading as a maid, by the gods, of course her clothing hadn't been proper for her rank.

Voice pitched like a mother speaking to an errant child, Sidjehuti asked, "Do you wish to go to the dinner as you are?"

"Of course not." Tuya didn't find the idea of allowing the two strange maids to help her change clothes appealing, but neither was facing a court full of people barefoot, in the filmy nightgown.

"Good. Better to submit before the queen's maid summons the rabisu to assist." Sidjehuti was matter of fact. "He waits outside the door."

Shivering, Tuya moved away from the wall into the center of the room to allow the ladies to work. The younger maid went to the baskets on the floor and took off the lids, revealing an assortment of clothing in one, makeup in another, and sandals and a cloak in the third. When Tuya was dressed and her hair arranged in a style mimicking the queen's elaborate tresses as much as possible, the maids painted her face with the same stylized white powder and vivid colors the queen had worn.

Tuya felt she must represent a sad imitation of Ninkurra's regal glory. Perhaps the effect was intentional, so no one could outshine the queen. The clothing was uncomfortable to her, the ruffles falling about her knees and lower legs were an unfamiliar irritant, and the drape kept sliding off her shoulder.

The maids gathered up their cases of makeup, the brushes and other implements, packing them in the baskets, talking quietly to each other and laughing. Then the women left the room after a few final remarks to Sidjehuti.

"What was so amusing?" Tuya practiced walking across the room in the dress and the oddly heeled sandals.

"Nothing flattering. The Isidu-Ur don't find the Egyptian standards of beauty particularly appealing."

"Are we waiting for something else?"

"The rabisu will come to escort us."

On the heels of Sidjehuti's words, the door was unbolted and a demon appeared, gesturing impatiently. The translator indicated for Tuya to precede her into the hall. One rabisu led the way, with a second following Tuya and her companion. Her cell was apparently in one tower of the building, as they descended quite a few stairs, crossed through a hall, and entered what appeared to be a second building. Soft music played and a murmur of voices filtered down the hall toward her. Hearing this, she pulled herself straighter and summoned a mental picture of how her own queen Ashayet moved. Always regal, graceful, as if nothing that happened could affect her. Tuya tried to adopt the same attitude.

The banquet room was huge, with space for many more tables and people than were actually present. Tuya crossed a broad expanse of tiled floor, following the demon as ordered, conscious of how the conversations died and all eyes were on her. The queen sat in an ornate chair at the exact center of the long rectangular table and beside her was a large gilded cage, containing a low, backless chair and a small table. A rabisu stood by, holding the cage door open. With horrified dismay, Tuya realized she was expected to occupy the space.

She came to a halt. "Strange hospitality you provide to your guests, Queen Ninkurra, expecting them to eat their meal in a cage, like a wild creature in a zoo, to be gawked at by their inferiors."

Sidjehuti gasped and gave the queen a wide-eyed look, but began translating.

Ninkurra waved one hand. "Was it not explained to you the entire purpose of this dinner is precisely for my court to see how fit you are to give the service?"

"By watching me sit behind bars?" Tuya made as if to turn. "I prefer to eat in my room."

There were gasps. Ninkurra slammed her fist on the table and uttered a short order. The closest rabisu picked Tuya up and carried her to the cage. She didn't struggle – she'd never expected to prevail, but she wasn't about to submit to what her captor wanted without at least objecting. The demon thrust her inside and locked the door with a growl before taking a position behind the queen. Sidjehuti sat on a low stool next to the cage and fussed with her skirt as if unhappy to be a part of the gathering.

Ninkurra spoke to her courtiers, ignoring Tuya.

In a low voice, Sidjehuti translated. "She says you've just proven how suitable you are, how much spirit you possess."

Tuya tossed her head. "I wasn't trying to make her happy."

"Nothing you can do will avert your fate," the translator said. "Resign yourself."

"My fate is to be what exactly?"

Sidjehuti blinked and glanced nervously at the queen before practically whispering her answer. "It isn't my place to say. I told you that before."

"All right, I'm not trying to get you in trouble." *Maybe I'm better off not to know what Ninkurra plans.*

The dinner was many courses, served by Egyptian servants. There was much drinking and merriment at the tables. Tuya's food was provided to her on trays, slid through an opening in the bars and removed the same way. She briefly toyed with refusing to eat but decided she needed her strength for whatever ordeals lay ahead.

As the night wore on, she found the music soothing, an odd mix of what she recognized as traditional Egyptian songs blended with music that must be of Isidu-Ur's culture. Several times when she glanced at the musicians, she found the harpist studying her while she waited to play her next portion of whichever song was underway. Always the woman hastily glanced away.

As if she wants to tell me something. But what can she know of me?

At length, the queen stood and launched into a long speech in her own language, which Sidjehuti dutifully translated. The gist of it was like a fairy tale in Tuya's opinion.

The story went on, all about lost kingdoms, escape from marauding enemies, settlement of hidden cities, and how the goddess had been kind enough to allow her beloved daughter Ninkurra to attain virtual immortality, so the princess could take care of her people for all time.

With dawning horror, Tuya realized Ninkurra believed what she was saying and so did everyone else in the room. She looked more closely at the queen. Could this woman actually be hundreds of years old? The Egyptian gods would never grant such a thing, not even to Pharaohs, who were Great Ones in their own right, but whose eternal life and pleasure took place in the duat, after death, not on earth.

The story changed tone, became mournful as Ninkurra talked about how the people's numbers dwindled despite her care for them, until the goddess heeded her daughter's pleas and sent a caravan to their door, lost in a sandstorm. Sidjehuti continued to provide a running translation of Ninkurra's words.

These poor people. Tuya was horrified at the idea of the caravan passengers and drovers prevented from going home, never to see their loved ones again. She had a terrible thought. If Egyptians died here, would they attain the afterlife? Did the gods count this as Egypt? Or was this still the domain of Ninkurra's long gone civilization and its gods? If *she* died here would she have a chance to have her heart properly judged?

Ninkurra kept talking, seeming to be inexhaustible. Her audience was rapt, attentive to her every word. Sidjehuti flicked a meaningful glance at Tuya as if to say, *pay close attention.*

"In order to renew the gift of the goddess, as you know, I have to partake of the energy of another. Someone young, high born, intelligent, with all the qualities a queen might need. Sadly the chosen one must die to pass the life force I need unto me. The Egyptians call it their ka, their soul. I sorrow for the taking of a life, but I must renew my youth and my powers in order to protect this city and you. When possible, I've obtained carefully selected candidates from the outside world, in order for me to also absorb information from the knowledge the sacrifice holds in her mind on how our enemies progress, what their rulers plan. Their language, their culture. I ask you now, my beloved people of Isidu-Ur, does this woman in our midst fit the description? Is she worthy to serve?"

A loud cheer and much applause erupted as the queen gestured at the cage. Tuya stared aghast at the group as the Halaqu aristocracy clamored for her death, no doubt in a horribly twisted ceremony. As her stomach rebelled she wished she hadn't eaten so much of the dinner.

The strikingly handsome man sitting next to Ninkurra rose and motioned for quiet. "I, Ekur-Sin, your high priest, hereby declare the woman has been found suitable. I've cast the omens, and the ceremony of renewal shall take place tomorrow night at moonrise at the temple. Praise to the goddess for allowing this miracle to occur, and praise to our queen for obtaining the right woman to serve our need."

"You people are crazy," Tuya shouted, standing and shoving her chair clattering against the bars of the cage. "I'm not dying to give my ka to your queen or anyone else. May the Great Ones curse your city, sending death on swift wings, carrying fire, floods, and pestilence!"

Unflustered by her prisoner's tirade, Ninkurra rose. "Escort the chosen one to her room. Let her not come forth again until the time for the ceremony." She walked away from the table without another glance at Tuya.

Tuya, for her part, was shouting the worst curses she could think of, hurling the oaths at the enemy while wishing they were spears rather than mere words.

The rabisu unlocked the cage and dragged her out, carrying her from the dining chamber as she wept from anger and fear. Sidjehuti hastened alongside the demon, her demeanor a little warmer than before. She patted Tuya's hand before stopping to allow the rabisu to climb the stairs to the cell alone. "I'll be with you tomorrow evening, to translate the ceremony as the high priest conducts the rituals."

"These Halaku people are insane," Tuya whispered, her voice harsh now and her throat aching. "If you were any kind of a decent human being, you'd help me escape."

The rabisu dumped her unceremoniously on the floor of her room and retreated, shutting the door with a bang. After another fruitless search of the room for anything, no matter how small, with potential to be a weapon, Tuya dragged herself to the balcony. She could think of no way to kill herself and thwart the queen's plan—even the bits of jewelry on the shelves had been stripped of any sharp pins or studs. Death by her own hand would have allowed her ka to survive, even if her soul was condemned to roam the wastes of the afterlife, never to enter the duat. Tuya huddled there for the remainder of the night, staring at the stars and praying for help.

Khian waited on a roof overlooking Merneith's home with an unobstructed view of the streets and houses. Ranefer was off hunting rabisu. Khian had charged

Nikare with investigating under cover of darkness what escape routes there might be from the city; bearing in mind they'd have two women with them.

Eager to hear her news, Khian watched the petite musician hurry down the path, swathed in her cloak, and into her house. He waited a half an hour for good measure, in case any sort of patrol or ambush was coming. Only when he decided the coast was clear did he descend from the spot and cross the ground to her house, keeping to the shadows, sword at the ready.

He entered her home soundlessly to find her seated in one of the chairs, staring into the fire. Her eyes were red as if she'd been weeping. Turning her head to stare at him, Merneith said, "Your lady's here, a prisoner in the palace. I saw her at dinner —she's in good health."

"Gods be praised." Khian sheathed the sword and studied her. "You seem under great distress. What haven't you told me?"

"The queen explained what purpose Tuya is to serve. I can only think this is black magic." She launched into a discussion of what had been revealed at the dinner. Halfway through, Khian got beer for both of them from the cooking alcove.

"Can any of this be true?" he asked. "Can the queen really be retaining her immortality by draining the kas of innocents like my Tuya?"

Merneith drained her mug and poured another. "Certainly those at the dinner believe her. After the gathering ended I asked one of my fellow musicians, whose mother is a priestess, what she knew of the ceremony. She told me after the goddess was kind enough to spare Ninkurra when her civilization fell to its enemies and give her the original extension of her allotted lifespan, the queen immediately charged her high priest at the time with finding a way to repeat the process. Apparently, Inanna never meant for Ninkurra to live forever, but somehow she's found a way."

"How often does she go through this horrific ceremony?"

"Every few hundred years, or so it seems. I'd never heard of it before today. Originally she took the women from the ranks of her own people, but tonight Ninkurra boasted at times she'd had others kidnapped from the outside world, as Tuya has been. She believes she absorbs knowledge along with the ka." Merneith frowned. "Even in my lifetime, I've seen the queen age. When I was young she was like a girl in her late teens, yet tonight she seemed much older than mere passage of years would cause, and the change has come on suddenly. I played at a harvest celebration for her court six months ago, and she was much younger in appearance then. Now she has white hairs threaded amongst the rest and all the white makeup can't hide deep wrinkles."

"Are the citizens all immortal here?"

Merneith shook her head. "The gift was to Ninkurra alone. The other Isidu-Ur are descendants of her original company."

"Fortunate the goddess wasn't even more generous." The white feather at Khian's wrist warmed as if to indicate he was missing something, a clue perhaps to a useful strategy, but he set the phenomenon aside for more practical concerns. "When is the ceremony?" He swallowed. "When is Tuya's death to occur?"

"The high priest said tomorrow night was propitious." Merneith blinked. "You know, my friend also told me in each generation the priesthood identifies a girl to be trained as Ninkurra's successor, in case the gift fails her, so they must not be as confident as she is."

"I'm surprised the queen allows it. Setting up a potential rival."

"The impression I received is the priests present it to her as training a new high priestess, which the girl does also become eventually." Merneith sat up in her chair with renewed energy. "The good news is my fellow musicians and I've been summoned to play the sacred music required at the ceremony, and we have a rehearsal in the temple chamber tomorrow morning. After that, I'll be able to give you detailed instructions on how to find the ceremonial site inside the building."

"Good news from the gods at last. Will the priests let you come home after the practice?"

She nodded. "Yes. The ceremony isn't until moonrise."

"I'll be watching for you, and we can make plans once you share what you learn."

"Will the others be with you tomorrow?" She spoke idly, toying with her hair and avoiding his eyes. "I freely admit the jackal warrior frightens me, but your friend Nikare is so…well spoken."

Khian could see her blushing. "We'll see. How many rabisu are there, does anyone know?"

"Legend says a limited contingent was granted to Ninkurra by the goddess as guards. I've no idea. There were five in the dining room tonight." Furrowing her brow, she paused. "I don't know that I've ever seen more than five in one place. But supposedly the rabisu patrol the tunnels so some would always be occupied elsewhere—"

"We entered the city through one of the main tunnels and met no one, much less a demon," Khian said. "Perhaps there are many fewer of them than anyone imagines. Like so much about this cursed place, the rabisu may not be what they seem either, or not entirely. Ranefer reported the one he killed wasn't as strong as expected. Perhaps time and this place are taking their toll on the demons as well. Few things outside the afterlife are meant by the gods to endure forever." He took comfort from the idea, while wondering how many of the gray demons Ranefer could take on at once, if he and Nikare fought by his side. Setting aside his mug, he rose. "Thank you for all your help. "

She clasped his hand, squeezing hard. "You won't forget your promise, to take me with you? After what I saw and heard tonight, I'm even more eager to be away from here. This city is cursed, unnatural."

Khian patted her hand and freed his own gently. "I'm a man of my word. If we escape, you will too. But I'm not leaving without Tuya. If she dies, I'll kill as many of these Isidu-Ur people as I can in revenge, starting with the queen, before I'm cut down. There'll be no thought of escaping then. Be ready to save yourself if it comes to that pass."

Merneith studied his face in the flickering firelight. "She means so much to you, this Egyptian lady?"

"She and I had much to say to each other." He swallowed. "*Still* have much to say to each other. Her station is above mine by more cubits than the Sphinx is tall—yet she's as firmly fixed in my heart as the stars are in the sky. I'll do everything I can to save her."

As dawn broke, his two companions rejoined him in the tumbled down house Khian had chosen as their hiding place. He briefed them on what Merneith had seen and learned. "I'm to go talk with her again at the noon hour, to hear the details of this temple, and the chamber where Tuya is to die." Soldier that he was, he kept his voice even but, in his heart, anger and fear mixed. He resolved yet again to rescue the lady and bring her safely home.

"I'd like to hear the account from her first hand," Nikare said. "Surely you trust our musician not to be setting us up for an ambush by now?"

Khian realized she'd become a trusted ally in his mind now. "Merneith was genuinely moved on Tuya's behalf, horrified by what she'd heard at dinner. I think it's a good idea if we plan our final strategy together." He asked Ranefer the question weighing on his mind. "How many of the demons can you take on at once and hope to kill?"

The jackal warrior grinned, showing off his impressive fangs. "My prowess and strength are in the hands of the Great One. I cannot die, since I was created by a god to serve him in this matter. But, if swarmed by too many, I might be unable to assist you. If these rabisu were as strong as legend credits them with being, matters might be otherwise. So far I've encountered none of that ilk."

"How many did you find in the night?" Khian asked.

Licking his lips and rolling his eyes, Ranefer said. "I dined on three more demon hearts."

"Sooner or later the queen is going to miss them," Nikare said.

"I think she's focused on this cursed ceremony." Khian continued sharpening his blade with a whetstone he'd found in the ruins of the house. "Besides, demons are magic, and who can say why they come or go? Certainly, Ninkurra can have no idea she faces a warrior of Anubis and two determined men sent by Pharaoh."

Nikare reached over and tapped the feather amulet on Khian's wrist. "And unknown other forces to be called upon, perhaps. 'Tis clear the goddess Mut favors you in this attempt to rescue Tuya."

"What escape routes have you located?" Khian changed the subject. He didn't believe he could rely on any external forces to assist them further at this point, now they were trapped inside this cursed and unnatural city. He and his companions had to help themselves.

"I believe the river is our best chance." Nikare rubbed a plum in his sleeve and bit into its juicy sweetness.

"I hadn't considered the idea." Khian stared at him.

Nikare swallowed a mouthful of the plum. "As you're an infantryman, I'm not surprised. I, however, have been a sailor a time or two when required by my assignments. There are small boats here. The locals seem to fish only in the backwaters, but they don't venture into the main current, which runs fast and powerful."

"The men probably stay out of the flow with good reason. Doesn't the river run under the earth once it leaves here? We could be sailing to our doom, eternally trapped below the desert. Or worse, if the cavern tightens and there's no room for a boat. Or even swimmers. We'd drown." He checked with Ranefer. "Can you swim?"

Head tilted, one pointed ear flicking as he pondered the issue, Ranefer reminded Khian of a dog. Or a jackal in truth. "We'll find out if it's a skill the Great One felt I needed."

"I doubt Tuya ever learned to swim and certainly Merneith has no idea of it." The plan didn't appeal much to Khian. Nikare was right – he did think first and foremost about battles taking place on the hard ground. To take to the river was against his nature.

"We don't know what condition Lady Tuya may be in." Nikare said, "As far as running to escape."

"The musician said she seemed fine, if understandably distraught over what the queen intends to do to her body and ka. She walked in under her own power." Khian worked on the blade a few moments longer, and the others let the silence stand while he considered.

He set the whetstone aside and sheathed the sword. "I tend to agree with you, however, that the likelihood of us fighting our way through the city and out one of the tunnels, traveling with two defenseless women, is small. And, once outside in the desert, we've no way to flee rapidly—even if I'd left the chariot horses tethered—and they survived - we can't all fit in the chariot." Khian sighed. "Your boat scheme has as much to recommend it as to argue against it."

"Granted. I stole a boat big enough for five of us if we crowd ourselves and hid it in the reeds just to the east of the docks," Nikare said. "So if we can make it from the temple to the water, which is a shorter route than across the entire city to any of the tunnels, we may stand a chance."

"This whole venture is a chance," Khian said. "Finding Tuya was more than I truly expected to accomplish, barring the further direct intervention of the gods."

"I think we're fortunate much of the city is abandoned, and the population appears to be on the decline, even with the addition of the caravan passengers two hundred years ago." Nikare took up the stone and honed his knife. "Ninkurra trusts too much to her demon guards and has few human soldiers."

CHAPTER NINE

Prior to the appointed hour for Merneith to arrive home from her rehearsal, Khian led his companions to her house, hiding again on one of the surrounding rooftops, to observe that she wasn't accompanied or followed. Once she appeared, and alone, the men made their way down from their perch and slunk through the shadows to her door, letting themselves into her house. She smiled shyly at Nikare as he entered.

Khian touched her arm to get her attention. "What news? Did you see Tuya again today?"

Shifting her focus to him, she shook her head. "No, there were only the musicians and a priest to tell us what he required tonight in terms of music. I don't know the song he wants well and will need to practice it this afternoon. I'm fainting from hunger, so let me prepare us a midday repast then I can draw you a map of the temple's interior."

"Seat yourself and rest, my lady." Nikare reached for the sack he'd been carrying. "Having nothing else to do this morning, I hunted small game and roasted my spoils in the fire pit of an abandoned house. Give me leave to make free of your kitchen, and I'll arrange the meat on a platter, along with vegetables filched from your garden and fruit I plucked from the abandoned orchard."

Speechless, Merneith blushed. "How thoughtful, too kind, of course anything you want in the house is yours."

"I had to while away the time somehow this morning and a man can only sharpen his weapons so much before ruining the edge." Nikare made an elegant bow, as if she were a noble lady at court. "You've been so helpful. This is a tiny gesture of repayment."

"I'll get the beer." Khian followed Nikare into the alcove.

The Medjai gave him a sidelong look as Khian located enough mugs and the beer pitcher. Raising one eyebrow, Nikare said, "Do I detect you wishing to make an observation, my captain?"

Khian shook his head. "If you want to take time to court a woman in the midst of this life or death situation, who am I to criticize? She's been a tremendous help, with more to come."

"There's always time to make graceful overtures to a lovely woman." Nikare whistled a bit as he broke the meat into chunks.

"Be careful not to draw her too deeply into your gods-given charm," Khian said. "She probably lacks the experience and sophistication of the ladies you're used to trading innuendoes with in Thebes. She may not know it's a game."

Nikare set the knife down with great deliberation and faced Khian. "And how do *you* know I'm playing a game?"

"I grow famished," Ranefer said in a raised voice. "Is there food coming or must I go hunting rabisu again for my next meal?"

Laughing, Nikare hoisted the platter and walked past Khian. "Impatient one, good food is worth waiting for."

Merneith made quick work of her lunch then rose to find a sheet of papyrus and a reed pen with which to draw her map of the temple. She proceeded to sketch the building in with rapid strokes and great detail.

"Your memory is exceptional," Khian said in admiration, watching over her shoulder.

Merneith laughed. "A musician must have a nimble memory, to recall all the songs a demanding audience might require. There, that's as much as I can give you." She pushed back from the table to give the men more room to study her drawing.

"I should add the temple was deserted for the most part. We Egyptians worship our own Great Ones in small spaces the original caravan travelers established, in our portion of the city. No grand temples. There were a few Isidu-Ur in the central area, here, but as we climbed the stairs to the top floor, where Tuya will be taken tonight, we passed only one or two priests. I observed no one in the adjoining halls."

"Except for their immortal queen, the Halaqu people seem to be dying off," Nikare said. "Do they intermarry with the Egyptians?"

Walking away from the group, she went to the kitchen. "Not often. It's not encouraged."

There was an odd tone in her voice. Khian wondered if she might have had hopes at one point of wedding a man from the ruling class. A broken affair would explain why she dwelt alone out here in the abandoned houses. *Another reason for her to help us as a means of escape.* Rubbing his hand over his unshaven face and grimacing, he focused on Tuya's predicament. "Two altars in the ceremony chamber?"

A fresh pitcher of beer in her hand, Merneith rejoined their company. "Yes, but oddly shaped." After setting the pitcher on the side table, she pointed at the map again. "We musicians will be here, in this alcove off to the side. The chamber isn't large so there can't be too many people in attendance tonight."

"Good for our purpose." Khian studied the first floor of the temple again. "No other way in than straight through the public worship space? The lack of alternate access points could be a problem."

"There must be another door," Nikare said. "The priests would want their own, private access." Raising one eyebrow as if reviewing old memories, he said with a chuckle, "In my experience the priesthood wishes to keep themselves apart and mysterious."

Merneith bit her lip. "I'm sorry—I saw no other entrance."

The Medjai flashed her a grin. "We'll scout the area, no problem."

"Once we get inside, by whatever means," Khian said, holding onto his patience as the flirtatious byplay continued, "We can ascend to the level below the ceremonial chamber and hide in one of these side halls you passed. From the size of the building, there must be other rooms up there on the second floor. And if few Isidu-Ur residents frequent the place, we can probably go undetected until moonrise, barring an unfortunate chance encounter."

"Unfortunate for them." Ranefer licked his chops, and his voice had a growl to it once more.

"We're to play a fanfare to the goddess, to initiate the ceremony." Merneith looked at her harp in the corner. "That can be your signal. There won't be any music prior to the fanfare. Which reminds me, I must practice."

"We'll be on our way soon, and the next time you see us will be in the temple chamber, gods willing." Khian rolled up the map and stuffed it into his belt. "I can't thank you enough for your help."

"Get me out of this cursed city and we'll be even." Jaw clenched, Merneith let her gaze travel over the interior of her house, lingering on the musical instruments. "Maybe Pharaoh will gift me a new harp in appreciation, and I can make my living in the Black Lands."

"If you have anything small you wish to take—a piece of jewelry perhaps—conceal it in your robes or on your person tonight. We won't be returning here," Khian said.

"And I'll buy you the harp if Pharaoh won't." Nikare's vow was made with a laugh. He drew his belt knife from its sheath and offered it to her. "Freshly sharpened. You might need this tonight."

Although she reached out to take the blade by the ivory hilt, Merneith recoiled. "I've no experience with knives, other than cutting reeds to make pens."

"I'll feel better if you have some means of defense." Nikare's face was set in serious lines.

Khian remembered the dainty knife they'd found in the hut with Anen's body. Having a weapon hadn't helped Tuya much, but he held his tongue on the issue. Picking up his beer mug, he said, "May the gods bless us and smile upon our efforts tonight."

The others, including Merneith, hastily grabbed their cups and clinked them against his.

Safely hidden in an empty room on the second floor of the temple, with a good view of the stairs, Khian was restless. He tried to discipline himself, set his mind to thinking only of the military nature of the attack they were going to be launching soon, but his thoughts kept circling back to Tuya. She might be injured in the close quarters of the ceremonial room. "My first priority will be to free her," he said in a low voice to Nikare.

"Yes, so you've told us more than once." The Medjai rested a hand on his shoulder. "We haven't come so far to lose your lady now."

As he heard voices Khian motioned sharply for silence. Shepherded by a young priest, the party of musicians ascended the stairs, Merneith in the center. She kept her eyes focused on the stairs, he was relieved to see, giving no sign of awareness that he and his men were hiding there. After the group passed the level on which Khian was hiding, a door creaked open above and no sound of it closing again. "Be ready," he whispered. "The priests should bring Tuya soon."

The next group to come up the stairs a few moments later was the queen's party. Khian stared at her with interest, noting the white hairs mixed in with the glossy black in her elaborate hairstyle, and there were definitely wrinkles under the stark makeup. She was excited and laughing at a remark the high priest made in their language.

Khian grimaced. "Eager to get the ceremony underway, may the gods rot her soul."

"I counted three more priests, two human guards, and one rabisu," Nikare said. "Plus a lady-in-waiting. Or maybe the extra woman was the apprentice 'just in case' heir apparent?"

"The guards and the demon are our main concerns," Khian said. "The priests appear overly well fed and soft, not likely to put up a fight. Women, of course, can surprise you in a fight, so watch your backs."

"I saw no weapons other than what the guards carry," Nikare added. "But in the worst case everyone in the group could have a concealed knife and know how to use it."

Khian appreciated the Medjai's caution. "The odds aren't too bad if we stay focused and eliminate the trained combatants quickly. We grab Tuya, and we get out of there, head for your boat and trust ourselves to the water."

Breakfast had been brought to her, but Tuya remained on the balcony, and no one bothered her. When she was sure the room was empty, she wandered into the chamber and picked at the food.

Knowing this was the day she was to die, no hint of appetite disturbed her belly. She took her choices outside and tipped a bit of the beer through the lattice, with a prayer for Mut, even though she doubted the Great One could hear her, locked in this place so far from Thebes.

As she forced herself to eat a hard roll and a few grapes, she daydreamed about Khian. The captain had been on her mind quite a bit during the long night. Regrets mostly, not confined to her stupidity in not asking him to go with her to ransom Anen, but also that she hadn't made more of an effort to know him better. "Closer acquaintance was my plan for the general's dinner."

A person always assumed there'd be plenty of time for everything and then the god Shai laughed and turned the world upside down on one. "I should have heeded your warning about my life and been much more determined," she said, addressing the goddess she served. She now believed Mut must have sent Khian into her life, one last chance to avoid the rutted path of aloneness, and she'd failed. If she and Khian had been a couple, even temporarily, by the time the ransom note for Anen was sent, she'd have asked the captain for advice, she was sure.

At the very least, even if she'd been kidnapped despite seeking Khian's counsel, he would have cared, would have tried to rescue her. Tuya was sure Khian was the kind of man not to easily give up on a woman close to his heart. Could she have been that woman, if they'd had more time? Or if she hadn't squandered the opportunity?

She brushed away tears. He was kind, strong, observed the principles of ma'at… and handsome. She'd felt relaxed, safe and happy when she was with him, even when she was momentarily annoyed at his high-handedness. "May I meet him in the afterlife," she whispered.

But she immediately chided herself for selfishness. Surely a man as exemplary as Khian had women at home interested in becoming mistress of his house once his service to Pharaoh was done. He wouldn't walk a solitary path just because he'd met Tuya a few times, nor would she wish such a fate on him.

He deserved a wife and children. Happiness.

The morning sun was warm, even with the odd shade patterns created by the lattice, and she drowsed, not having slept at all during the night. The dreams were confused, fragmentary like an old papyrus deteriorating unread. She dreamt Khian was calling to her, trying to reach her, but in vain. When she awakened Tuya had fresh tears on her cheeks.

Voices echoed in her cell room, and she knew the time had come. Determined to be brave and pass into the afterlife with dignity and hope, as an Egyptian woman should, Tuya rose to her feet. She smoothed the crumpled dress from the night before. *I won't give the Isidu-Ur the satisfaction of reducing me to a sobbing puppet, begging in vain for my life.*

Sidjehuti stepped onto the balcony. "The maids are here to bathe and dress you."

"Very well." Tuya moved past her, entering the room. "Tell them no makeup today, and no one is touching my hair. I'll not be made into a shabby duplicate of your queen. I'll go to my death as myself."

"I—I'm not sure that's possible—"

Pivoting on one heel, Tuya gave her the look Queen Ashayet might have bestowed on anyone who disagreed with her orders. "This is the one condition I insist upon. I will have my dignity."

The interpreter swallowed hard and spoke to the maids, who clearly wanted to argue.

Tuya shed the dress and moved toward the bathing area, in an alcove off her main room. "Tell them they waste time, and the queen will be angry."

Apparently, no one could argue with the truth of her statement. The bath was refreshing, no matter the circumstances. Tuya stood patiently while the maids dressed her in a long white gown, with the same oddly shaped petal ruffles, ever so slightly edged in red, and a red drape over her right shoulder.

The door opened with no warning and a priest entered, followed by one of the gray demons. "It's time to proceed to the temple," he said in awkward Egyptian.

"All right." Tuya slid her feet into the strange, heeled sandals and stared at him. "What are we waiting for?"

The priest dangled a pair of golden shackles in his hand, giving them to the demon guard with an order Sidjehuti didn't bother to translate.

The rabisu moved behind her, grabbing her wrists and securing them in the tight-fitting cuffs. Then he shoved her, causing Tuya to stumble toward the door. It was hard to regain her balance with her hands bound behind her back, and the priest had to catch her to keep her from falling. Keeping his hold on her elbow, evidently deciding she was going to need more help, he led her from the room.

The demon and the translator followed. She was taken down a long flight of stairs and outside into the cool night. She gazed once at the stars above, longingly, hoping to see a late flying vulture or a falling star or other sign she was to have help, or mercy at least. But the sky remained clear.

The temple was many cubits away from the wing of the palace where she'd been held captive, but there seemed to be no animal drawn conveyances in this city, nor litters, so she walked with her captors, accompanied by guards carrying torches to light the way, despite the generous moonlight. There was no crowd, no watchers, and the whole place seemed deserted to her. Tuya shivered—and not merely from the chill of the night air. Isidu-Ur was a city out of its time, possibly even cursed.

Eventually, the procession reached the steps of the temple, which were brightly lit by huge oil lamps. The priest cast an anxious glance at the moon and gave the rabisu a curt order. The demon flung Tuya none too gently over his shoulder and carried her up the sweeping stairs and inside the building.

"Tell him to put me down," she said to Sidjehuti. "I'll go quietly if I'm allowed to walk on my own."

The translator spoke to the priest, who seemed inclined to disagree as the group crossed a vast open space, with many statues and wall paintings Tuya had no interest in looking at. None of these ancient deities were hers and would take no interest in helping an Egyptian escape the fate awaiting her.

When they reached another stairway located beyond the altars, the priest addressed the demon more sharply, who grunted and set Tuya on her feet.

"Honor your promise," the priest said in an angry hiss.

"I've scant incentive to do anything you request," Tuya retorted but since she wanted to stay on her own two feet in case there was an opportunity to escape or to throw herself off the upper floor, she didn't attempt any physical rebellion now. *Lull them.*

He brushed past them to ascend first. Tuya was next, with Sidjehuti behind her and the rabisu and the guards bringing up the rear. The other guards stayed below, taking positions to block the staircase, in case anyone was rash enough to be curious and seek entry.

As she ascended the stairs Tuya still felt icy cold, calm, detached, as if this wasn't actually happening to her. Having her hands bound was uncomfortable, but she was sure worse trials lay ahead. There was a pricking between her shoulder blades as if she was being watched—by curious priests hiding in the corridors they passed on each floor perhaps?

She entered the ceremonial chamber to find the queen and her high priest already waiting. Incongruously, the musicians from dinner the night before were seated in an alcove, instruments at the ready. Viewing the twin altars waiting side by side in the center of the room, her resolve slipped. She faltered and the priest exerted pressure to keep her walking until she stood beside the one to the left.

Sidjehuti took up a position against the wall but close enough to allow her softly murmured translation to fall upon Tuya's ears all too clearly.

The high priest recited a prayer or an incantation that was so much gibberish to Tuya, even with the Egyptian meaning from Sidjehuti. Her head was spinning, she could hardly breathe, and her body felt as if her ka was going to flee at any moment, tearing its way from her heart and soaring to freedom. *I pray it be so.*

Two other priests came forward carrying huge ceramic vases, painted with wedge-shaped symbols executed in red and black. The men poured the contents into the waiting altar next to her. Tuya realized the twin altars were shaped like shallow bathtubs or coffins. The liquid was milky white, with bits of flowers and leaves floating on top. The scent was pleasant at first, if a bit cloying, but then the notes underneath reached her nose and she gagged. Some spice or other ingredient was putrid, speaking of death and decay. The priests continued to add more liquid until the fluid slopped over onto the floor and drained away through a channel cut in the tile.

The high priest stepped to the altars and inspected the fluid, chanting under his breath and sprinkling a brown powder onto the surface from a pouch at his belt. He examined a pipe running from one altar to the other, apparently stoppered for the moment, as Tuya noticed the basin she stood next to was at a slightly higher level. The man addressed her and Sidjehuti translated for the priest, "You will be disrobed and placed into the sacred elixir of eternity, drawing it into your lungs instead of the air. Queen Ninkurra will take her place in the other altar and, at the appointed moment, I will allow your ka to leave your body and flow into hers through the channel.'"

"Your service will be complete." The queen drew nearer to the altars, running her hand over the lip of the basin destined to be her macabre bathing pool. "And I'll rise renewed for another span of centuries."

"You're going to drown me in that nauseous bath?" Tuya shrank back, but the priest at her side kept her in place.

A crash of sound erupted from the harp as the musician reacted, either to Tuya's protest or to the idea of what was going to happen.

The high priest spun on his heel and shouted angrily at the woman.

From his place of concealment, Khian had gotten one precious glimpse of Tuya ascending the stairs as her procession passed his level. She looked calm, but he sensed her underlying terror, expressed in the tense set of her face, the rigidity of her shoulders. *Soon, soon,* he promised her silently. Then he waited, on the sharp edge, ready for action and combat. Yet no music sounded.

"This is taking too long." Nikare voiced the concern Khian felt. "Maybe the priest switched the music, or decided not to have accompaniment."

A long, discordant note from the harp sounded, echoing in the stairwell. Definitely not music, but Khian had had enough. He burst from the room where they'd lain in wait and charged up the short flight of stairs to the ceremony room, Nikare and Ranefer on his heels. Yelling an Egyptian war cry invoking the god Horus, he plunged through the open doorway and slashed his sword through the neck of the first guard, severing the man's head from his shoulders before the soldier even knew he was there.

Abandoning all caution, Khian sprinted across the room to where Tuya stood. The high priest scrambled out of his path, but the other man failed to move fast enough. Khian cut him down and caught Tuya to him with his free arm. "Are you all right?"

"You came for me!" Her eyes glistened with tears, and she nestled close to him, resting her head on his chest.

He brushed a kiss over her hair. "Stay behind me."

A rabisu charged at them. Ranefer was busy beating one into submission in the central area of the chamber, raking its body with his fearsome hind claws, his jaws buried in the creature's neck. Nikare rushed to assist Khian, moving from the spot where he'd done battle with the other human guards. Together, the two men drove the demon away from where Tuya stood, trading slashing blows with the creature until Ranefer was done with his first kill and came to assist. Launching himself onto the rabisu's back, he dug in with his massive black talons, lowering his head to clamp his fangs into the neck. Khian and Nikare retreated as Ranefer wrestled the demon to the floor and broke its neck. Tuya gave a small shriek but quickly stifled it.

Khian turned to where Merneith was unfastening Tuya's shackles with keys taken from the dead priest while another Egyptian woman cowered to the side. The golden cuffs fell to the floor as he reached Tuya, giving her a quick, hard embrace, relieved to have her safe within his arms. "We're leaving. Now." He took Tuya's elbow just as a resounding crash echoed through the room.

"No one is leaving." Queen Ninkurra stood at the door which she'd apparently shut. "I will have my renewal – this woman must serve me."

"You're insane," Tuya said.

"Where is my high priest?" Ninkurra asked, her tone making it clear this was a rhetorical question. She gestured around the chamber. "He's gone to fetch reinforcements—the rest of the rabisu and my soldiers. There are secret ways into and out of this room, known only to my priest and me. The door itself answers only to my command so you're trapped for the moment. But when Ekur-Sin arrives, you'll be outnumbered and slaughtered. She *will* die this night to serve me."

"I'll kill myself before I'll let you steal my ka." Tuya snatched Khian's belt knife and took a step forward before he caught her free hand.

"My rabisu will kill your champions, and you *will* die to serve me."

"You'll die easily enough." Nikare threw his dagger with pinpoint accuracy but, before it could reach the queen, the weapon slowed and stopped in midair.

As Khian stared in appalled disbelief, the knife fell to the floor with a clunk as if the blade had struck a stone wall.

"Immortal, remember?" Ninkurra laughed. "I'll be the only one left alive in here if my orders aren't obeyed. I may be in need of refreshing my gift from the goddess, but I still have enough power left to defeat you, Egyptians." She stepped forward to grab the knife before anyone could stop her.

The feather amulet on Khian's wrist grew hot, tingling against his skin. He raised his arm, the movement catching Tuya's eye, and she stepped forward with a cry. The leather thong unwrapped itself like a snake uncoiling and the feather, glowing red, flew to her outstretched hand.

The instant the feather came to her hand, power flowed through Tuya's body, and she knew she could ask for help now and be granted the boon. "I call upon the mother, the Great One Mut, come to help us in this dire moment," she said, her voice ringing in the chamber.

A hot desert wind blew through the room, although there were no windows, only a skylight above. Khian and his group drew closer together behind her as the torches flickered and the smell of the Nile lotus grew strong.

"I come to assist, my daughter, now you've identified the place where the evil dwells." The voice was beautiful, bell-like, and seemed to be coming from everywhere at once.

Majestic, glowing white wings folded, the goddess Mut stood in the center of the room, Anubis a few paces behind her, and another woman next to him. The Great Ones were easily ten feet tall and majestic in their beauty, glowing with power.

Ninkurra cried out, staring fixedly at the woman behind Mut, who was dressed in a more elaborate version of what she herself wore, wearing a golden crown patterned like delicate leaves and draperies of sheer fabric that shimmered. "Inanna."

Tuya realized the Isidu-Ur goddess, if it was she, was less fully present than the two Egyptian Great Ones. She could see through the older goddess from one moment to the next, as if Inanna was a flickering flame.

Mut held up one hand, freezing the queen in her tracks. "I summoned your mother goddess from her place in the far removed afterlife, for her time is long past, as is yours, Ninkurra Azimua. I wished my sister Inanna to see what became of her impulsive gift of temporary immortality to a beloved mortal. This is not the outcome the goddess intended, and I believe you knew that all along, mortal woman. As you schemed to extend the gift you were given, and sacrificed the kas of others to achieve your theft of time, you know you were in the wrong. You took sacred knowledge never meant for you." She extended one hand, palm up, and spoke a word of power. The tops of the two altars tipped, and the noxious fluid meant for Tuya cascaded to the floor, miraculously disappearing as it touched the tiles so not one drop was left. The altar stones themselves cracked in a million pieces then crumbled to dust.

Ninkurra screamed in fury and struggled to leave the spot where she stood, but it was as if her legs were paralyzed.

Mut extended her other hand to the shadow of Inanna. Anubis stepped aside, and the older goddess solidified and became as real as the Great Ones for a moment. Her large brown eyes were sad as she gazed at Ninkurra. Although Tuya didn't see her lips move, a new voice was heard in the room, speaking in Isidu-Ur, which Sidjehuti translated in a shaking voice.

"I loved you, my beautiful daughter, and I granted you the gift you requested, folded you inside the wings of my butterfly, that you might emerge renewed, to lead your people to safety in this place where we now stand. Two hundred years I granted you, time to get the city established, time to find happiness, marry, and bear children to follow you in the rule of this place. Time to create one tiny corner of the world where our life might continue and grow, in spite of what the enemies of your father could do. They might obliterate his name, my name, and his civilization from the memory of man and woman but you were to ensure a fragment remained. This was your prayer, and this I did grant, partly of my own vanity, I admit. Even as I knew my time was over, I gave this one final gift to you, my favorite of all the children of our proud nation. It was wrong, for even the gods have their appointed time and must move on." The voice grew stern. "But you understood the terms of my boon and you violated them, as my sister of the earth has shown me tonight."

Ninkurra fell to her knees, casting aside the knife and raising her hands in supplication. "Please, I beg of you, one final renewal. Let me have time to set this all to rights."

"You've had ample time and more," Inanna said. "The time is done."

A crack of thunder boomed directly overhead, and the room plunged into absolute darkness for a heartbeat.

When the lamps flickered into life again, Tuya blinked. The Great Ones and Inanna were gone. In the spot where Ninkurra had knelt, there was a giant, bright green chrysalis, big enough to hold a person within its shining, tightly closed folds. As Tuya watched, the pod opened, the lips unfurling with reluctance, sticky, as if coated in honey. Hundreds of butterflies exploded into the room, swirling higher and higher in a mad spiral until the swarm flew out the skylight and were gone.

Khian went to the now shrunken and faded pod and toed it with his sandal. "No sign of her body."

"I guess her goddess decided to grant her wish," Tuya said, repressing an urge to laugh hysterically. "One final renewal."

Khian came to her, taking her in his arms tenderly. "Are you sure you're all right? I was so afraid for you, all this time."

"I can't believe you followed me here." And then she kissed him, relishing the safe harbor of his strong arms after so many days of terror.

"I'd sworn not to ever give up until I found you," Khian said. "But now we need to escape."

Emphasizing his point, there was pounding at the door.

"Anyone have an idea where these hidden exits the late queen boasted about might be?" Nikare asked.

Merneith pointed at an intricately painted section of the wall. "The priest let himself out here while the rest watched your jackal warrior fight the rabisu. I didn't see what he did to trigger the door, though. One moment he was standing there, and the next he was gone."

Ranefer prowled over to the section, putting his nose to the paint, and sniffed. "Here." He straightened and pushed on a section dense with calligraphy. The wall slid aside smoothly, revealing a narrow, dark opening.

Grabbing an oil lamp from its stand, Khian stuck his head into the space and reported to his companions. "A steep and narrow stairway. I was afraid we might meet an attacking force coming up, but now I judge no sane commander would take the risk. Nikare, take point and, once you emerge from the staircase, head for the agreed upon rendezvous."

Nikare slid past the open section of the wall.

Khian took Tuya's hand and led her to the door. She hesitated. "What about you?"

"Ranefer and I'll bring up the rear." He grinned. "You won't lose us, I promise." Kissing her on the cheek, he said, "Go quickly." Next, he pulled Merneith to the space. "Second thoughts?" he asked as he handed her another of the small oil lamps.

She shook her head. "Far too late for those. I possess no misgivings, only joy at leaving with you." The musician gave an exclamation of dismay once she was in the dark staircase but, as he heard nothing more, he assumed she was making her descent.

"I'll bring up the rear," Ranefer said. "You go next."

Khian shook his head. "It's my job—I'm in command."

"And I cannot be killed by any being here. As the ineffectual rabisu have proven over and over since we arrived." The jackal warrior bared his fangs as the pounding on the outer door resumed in earnest. "Go, my friend."

Without further argument, Khian swept the chamber with a final glance. The translator was huddled on the floor, her face covered with the draperies of her dress as if to blot out all that had happened. He tapped her on the shoulder. "Did you wish to come with us?"

She shook her head without looking at him. "This is my home."

The sole remaining woman was most likely the one chosen to apprentice to Ninkurra. Khian assumed she'd just become queen. "A word of advice," he said to her, catching her eye as she glared across the room at him. "The time has passed for your people, and Pharaoh rules the Black Lands, supported by our gods, as you've clearly seen this night. Stay here in your bubble of a world and be left alone. Venture forth to make a true treaty and the Great One might listen. But don't entertain any ideas about recreating the past glories." He pointed his sword at her. "No more raids on caravans, no more kidnappings. Consider yourself warned."

Feeling he'd done his duty on behalf of Pharaoh, he entered the staircase and made quick work of descending, one hand on the wall to guide him in the darkness. Above, he heard Ranefer forcing the hidden panel to a closed position from the inside then heavy steps as the jackal followed him.

When he reached the bottom, the door stood open, and he sprinted into the moonlight, running full tilt downhill, toward the river, which glinted enticingly. He saw the figures of Nikare and the two women making the best time they could, not far ahead. The street was deserted, but he heard shouts behind him from the temple.

Ranefer caught up to him, running easily, not at all fatigued by the deadly combat he'd waged in the tower a few moments before. "The enemy will pursue us."

"Not onto the river."

"We must reach the boat—there'd be no mercy for you and the other humans if the locals do catch up." Ranefer took a glance behind him as the road curved gently. "The rabisu come. I'll drop back and engage them—don't wait for me."

Khian redoubled his pace as arrows struck the road on either side of him. A lucky shot clipped his shoulder, inflicting a slashing pain, but he kept his speed steady. Behind, he heard Ranefer giving voice to truly horrendous howls, challenging the demons to pay attention to only him. *I wish the Great Ones had seen fit to remove the rest of the rabisu as well as taking Ninkurra's immortality.* But the Great Ones were never too generous with their assistance – humans were always expected to do their part. Ahead, Nikare and the women working frantically to push the boat into the water.

He ran full tilt into the shallows, grabbing the opposite side of the boat from Nikare. "Tuya, Merneith, get in and duck down. There are archers coming."

Khian helped boost one first then the other over the side and into the bottom of the stolen boat. Tuya lingered a moment, exclaiming at his wound.

Khian urged her to keep moving. "It's not serious – you can bind it for me later," he said as he resisted the current pulling at his lower body and the small craft's hull.

Nikare got himself up and over the boat's side and deployed an oar. "Where's Ranefer?" the Medjai yelled.

"Delaying the demons. We're not to wait for him." The bottom went out from under Khian's sandals unexpectedly and only the fact he had a tight grip on the boat saved him. As the craft picked up speed, he swung one leg over the gunwale and managed to lever himself into the boat with a thud, landing between the women. "Can we make this thrice damned thing sail any faster?" He could hear arrows hitting the water with small splashes and one lodged in the side of the boat too close to Tuya for Khian's comfort.

"If we get to the main current, we'll be fine. Take the tiller, would you?" Nikare worked the paddle, first on one side, then the other.

Khian moved to the stern, stepping carefully over Tuya, and deployed the wooden tiller, which was held to the boat by sturdy rope rather than being affixed. In vain he searched for a more reliable stone tiller on a rope, to cast overboard, but the boat wasn't equipped with one. From his vantage point at the stern, hoping for a sign of Ranefer, he watched the shore grow farther away.

The boat lurched, and one of the women screamed a bit as the main current grabbed the hull like a twig in the Nile. The boat shot forward. Nikare came to join Khian at the tiller, to add his strength to steering a straight course toward the spot where the torrent exited the Isidu-Ur valley.

"Can you keep watch at the bow, my lady?" he said to Tuya. "Warn us of any obstacles?"

"Of course." She scrambled to the bow and peered beyond the crude figurehead. "The river runs clear."

"So far so good then." Nikare's triumphant grin was wide. "We might survive this mad adventure yet, my friends."

The boat moved past the city's waterfront at a rapid speed. Much of the area was in ruins, like the outer neighborhoods. "The new queen will have her challenges. Hopefully, she'll be too busy to bother anyone in her city's vicinity. No more seizing caravans."

Merneith sat up and wrung water from her dragging skirts. "My people may feel more encouraged to attempt to leave now the immortal queen has perished. Of course, the new queen and the high priest may well try to keep word of exactly what happened a secret." She searched in the shadows at the bottom of the boat. "I think we'd better bail. This craft seems leaky." She found a tightly woven basket of reeds and began pouring water scooped from the excess sloshing over their feet out into the river.

"Sidjehuti should have come with us," Tuya said from the bow.

"Who?" Khian asked.

"The translator. She wasn't a friend but neither was she an enemy. The high priest isn't likely to leave her alive after tonight. I wish I'd encouraged her to flee."

"Eyes on the river, please, my lady," Khian said. "Your concern for the woman does you credit, but I spared a moment to ask if she wished to accompany us and she refused. Those who hesitate are often lost, in battle and in other extreme moments."

Tuya turned away from him and stared at the river as requested. She gave a little shriek. "I see waves and whitecaps at the cavern entrance as if there are rocks. We need to approach obliquely, with care."

"Good advice," Nikare said, struggling with the tiller, "But impossible to execute. The current has us in its claws."

Khian moved to the oar and, working together, the two men did their best to steer the boat out of the mad rush of the central current. They had scant success.

"There's a grate," Tuya cried. "The tunnel mouth is completely blocked."

The boat struck the grate with a thump and remained there, held by the inexorable current. Fortunately, the craft seemed stable enough for the moment, but Khian had misgivings about its ability to remain in one-piece long. He joined Tuya at the prow and stared at the obstacle. "We're not getting through this barrier."

"The Isidu-Ur authorities must have constructed it during a dry season, when the flow ebbed," Merneith said. "To prevent escapes such as the one we're attempting. What do we do now?"

"Waiting for the next dry season to occur isn't an option," Nikare said with his usual flippancy. "Nor is trying to swim to shore and heading for a tunnel. Not in this raging current."

"I can't swim," Tuya said.

"Nor can I." Merneith echoed.

"I can, and I'm going to have to make the attempt." Khian stood with care and divested himself of his sword and belt. "We've got no other option."

Tuya gestured at the water. "Unless the Great Ones assist you, you'll never make it, especially if you're trying to tow us, or even worse, tow the boat."

Nikare pointed. "We might have the help you were mentioning."

Ranefer was swimming strongly to them, seeming to ride the current as much as stroke through it. "Problem?" he said when he arrived, looping one arm over the side of the boat to hold himself in place.

"A grate over the opening." Khian gestured. "We're about to make the attempt to swim ashore."

"And meet the enemy in force," the jackal soldier said. "The priests are rousing the entire city." He worked his way along the boat, hand over hand, to get closer to the grate. "I'll look." Taking a deep breath, he released the boat and disappeared under the roiling surface.

A long moment later he resurfaced, shaking his head to send water droplets flying. "One portion seems rotted. I'm going to do what I can to shatter the weakest part of it then we might have an opening sufficient for the boat to pass.

Be ready." Taking a deep breath, the jackal soldier released the boat and dove under the water again.

"Can he possibly break the grate?" Tuya asked.

Khian shrugged. "The Great One Anubis sent him to aid us, and he's much more powerful than a human, so I have hope."

More arrows rained down from the shore.

"They're getting the range." Nikare ducked and covered Merneith to shield her from the deadly barrage. "Ranefer better succeed quickly or we'll be as full of quills as the desert hedgehog."

The boat surged and spun, going through the tunnel opening stern first, riding a wave of water as the grate was partially severed from the walls. A jagged remnant remained, hanging precariously above them as the boat slipped past and entered the large cave beyond. The current's speed was dizzying, much faster even than a chariot drawn by galloping horses. Khian knew he and Nikare should try to turn the boat, but at the moment there was nothing to do but hang on and try to keep the two women safely in the boat as well. The water raced through its channel, luckily with ample open space above their heads and to the sides, and curved gently as it pursued its well-worn course.

Khian hoped their luck held and prayed to Anubis to help his jackal warrior find a way to survive after his gallant effort to set them free.

CHAPTER TEN

Many cubits away from the city, the water slowed in its flow, and the men were able to correct the boat's orientation so the bow faced forward, as was proper. Nikare sat at the tiller, with Merneith at his side, talking in low voices. The caverns they sailed through were huge, with the ceiling lost to view entirely. Here and there the walls were speckled with light, as some moss or lichen clung to life and cast illumination on the scene, but for the most part the darkness was near absolute. The only sound was the rush of the river.

Tuya insisted on tearing a strip from the drape over her shoulder, which was dry enough, and bandaging Khian's wound while the boat traveled through a section of cave lit by the unusual plants.

"You did your treatment of my wound very neatly, my lady." He flexed his arm when she was done. "As good as an army physician could do on the battlefield."

Pleased by his praise, she curled herself into his embrace. Khian was warm, and she was shivering.

He held her close, and his heartbeat was steady under her ear. Strong and reassuring like the man himself. "Thank you for coming after me," she said. "I prayed so hard for help, but I didn't truly expect any. I didn't—I never dared to hope you'd be the one to save me."

"When Hemaka came to me with that cursed false ransom note," he said, "my only thought was to wish *you'd* come to me in the first place, trusted me to help."

"I'm sorry," she said, unable to tell from his tone if he was angry with her. "I can't tell you how many times I've regretted my impulsive choice to try to solve the problem alone, to keep anyone else from knowing about Anen. I should have trusted you."

"In the future," he said, running his fingers through her hair and massaging her scalp gently, which Tuya found indescribably calming, "I expect to be the first to hear of anything besetting you and will be the first to step in to help. Agreed?"

"No arguments from me." If she'd been a cat, she'd be purring under his caress, despite the dire circumstances.

"My second thought, hard on the heels of the first, was to reach your side and extricate you from the trouble I was sure you were in." He laughed. "I didn't expect the journey to be so long or so fraught with unnatural perils. You constantly amaze me, Lady Tuya."

"Is amazement a good thing?" she asked, hoping for reassurance.

"Very much so." He tilted her chin up so he could kiss her. "Life would never be boring in your company."

"Which is ironic and amusing to hear you say because before all this adventure arose like a sandstorm, the goddess warned me I'd allowed myself to sink deep into mire. She said I was seeking nothing but the comfort of a boring, safe life. I resolved to try to break from my too well-trodden path. I thought—" She bit her tongue and fell silent.

After a moment, he said, "Go on, what were you going to say?"

Relieved the boat was sailing through a darkened area of the cavern and her face was hidden, she said, "I hoped you might be the one to help me find a new path. Sent by Mut to open a different possibility."

"Your goddess said as much to me when we met," he said, his voice sounding neutral in Tuya's anxious ears.

"She gave you the amulet then? I wondered why a warrior would wear her feather, glad as I was to see it so I could petition her to intervene."

"I was her chosen champion," he said, voice bearing a note of pride. "But she asked me to accomplish a task I'd already set myself. Finding you and saving your life meant everything to me." Khian hugged her closer. "If we survive this situation and make it to Thebes, what do you see for the future?" His voice was quiet, deep as always.

Oddly reluctant to voice her vision of their shared future, she began tentatively. "You could remain in Thebes, become one of Pharaoh's Own—"

His laugh stopped her in mid-sentence. "Can you truly imagine me as one of their company? I'm an ordinary farmer, a small landowner from the Jackal Nome who got conscripted, assembled his men, and did his duty fighting for the Great One."

Compelled to argue in the face of his amusement, she said, "You've rescued me against all odds—well, you will have if we get back to Thebes—you have gold of valor, Nat-re-Akhte thinks highly of you—"

"Being in the elite company requires more than that." Again he interrupted, his voice patient and good humored. "Much more. Khenet, Sahure, Kamin, Tadenhut—all of them trained from early childhood to be warriors, to drive chariots, master the art of archery, triumph in any sword fight. They learned strategy while still wearing the braids of boys. I learned about crop cycles, when to plant, how to nurture livestock, the management of vineyards and orchards. The men I've named are the tip of the spear Pharaoh launches at his enemies. I could never aspire to be in their ranks—the desire isn't even in my heart. I long to return to my lands and the people there who look to me for protection and order, and apply my hands to the tasks I do best."

Thinking he didn't value himself highly enough, she had to protest again. "But you *are* a warrior—I saw you fight for me in Isidu-Ur. Pharaoh doesn't bestow gold of valor on farmers."

"Battling demons and priests to save your life was fueled by the strong feelings I have for you, for what I'd hoped we might find together, before this evil queen's plot stole you away. As far as the war, my men and I fought like demons and, due to many factors, including the grace of the gods, we managed not to get killed before General Marnamaret got there. We were lucky. The Great One can heap as many honors on me as he pleases, but I know the truth—I was in the right place at the right time and no personal valor was involved. Other than to stand and fight while I prayed for reinforcements." As the boat slid into another lighted area of the cavern, he turned her to face him. "Are you so determined then to remain in Thebes? To maintain your place at court and your spot as a priestess?"

"What else would I do?"

She didn't expect him to laugh and thought he didn't sound particularly amused, although his voice stayed pleasant. "Indeed. I've heard the stories of you as a lady determined to be the last person standing when the Great Ones descend into their tombs.

She'd no idea the court spoke of her in such terms and wasn't comfortable with the idea. "No, you have it all wrong. I struggle with change, with the idea of leaving all I have here, to take a risk—are you asking me to give my life at court up and go to the Jackal Nome with you?"

"No," he said. She was astonished by the firm tone in his voice. "I can see it's too soon to have the conversation. Clearly, you can't possibly imagine life there with me, and I can't imagine my life in Thebes as you've described it."

"Are we at an impasse then?" She felt close to tears, astonished her heart could feel so broken so soon after the joy of Khian saving her from death in the lost city.

"You give up too easily, my lady. I'm a man pursuing a goal I'm much invested in, and I haven't begun to play the game in earnest. Before I'm finished, I hope to create such desire in you to become the mistress of my house, the lady of my estate, that you'll be amazed you ever hesitated. The glories of Thebes will be as nothing to you." His easy laugh punctuated the remark, and she could tell he was teasing her. "And I don't need an oracle to tell me I need to know much more about you and what lies in your past to make you so resistant to change."

"And obviously I need to hear a paean to the joys of life in the Jackal Nome," she said, trying to carry off a flirtatious tone. "Probably more than one." Panic clawed at her gut. She was going to have to make a choice at some point—keep her life of comfort and certainty and lose Khian, or take a step into the completely unknown to be his wife.

"I have other methods of persuasion as well." He stroked her arm in a slow, sensuous manner and nipped at her ear lobe before kissing her neck.

She felt he'd embarked on a promising beginning, but Nikare chose the next moment to interrupt.

"The river's flow is diminishing," he said. "We're coming into a lake and, if my ears aren't lying to me, there's a waterfall at the other end. I doubt our fragile craft would survive the drop. Nor would we. I think we should land the boat on the upcoming beach and see if there's a way to climb to the surface. We've traveled a great distance to the east in this system of caverns."

"What makes you think we'd have any luck escaping the caves?" Khian asked, studying the broad expanse of flat, sandy riverbank ahead.

Nikare leaned over his shoulder to point. "Tell me those rays aren't daylight."

Sure enough, at the far end of the beach, Tuya could see shafts of light striking the sand, making it glitter like black crystals.

"If the light can get in," Nikare said, "we can get out."

The men landed the boat using the paddle and the tiller then handed the ladies from the small craft. Tuya found it hard to walk at first, her legs having gotten cold and numb in the cramped boat but, by leaning on Khian's strong arm, she was able to make her way toward the beacons of light.

At the base of the cavern wall, they stood staring upward where rosy daylight was clearly visible through an opening in the rocks.

"I'll go," Nikare said. "I'll let you know what I find up there." Studying the rock face for a moment, he selected his first handholds and places to set his feet then began a slow ascent toward the light. He had to descend and backtrack once or twice but, eventually, he'd climbed about fifty feet and disappeared from view.

"I hope he's found a way out," Tuya said. "But I'm not sure I can climb the cliff as he did. I'm not fond of heights."

"I'll be right there to help," Khian assured her. "And assist you as well, of course," he added, bowing to Merneith.

"I craved adventure in my life, since I was a young girl," the musician said, rubbing her hands together as if cold. "This has been much more than I bargained for but, once the gods grant a human's wish, there's no controlling the way the game sticks fall."

"So true." Tuya nodded. "We have to do the best we can."

Nikare reappeared far above, waving his arms and yelling down to them, "The way is clear to the outside. I'll come down and guide you on the best route to climb."

"I fear for him, attempting the trip twice," Merneith said. "It can't be safe."

"Nikare knows what he's doing. I think we should move back," Khian said. "In case he dislodges any loose rocks. I should have considered the danger when he ascended the cliff, but better late than never."

They withdrew to the vicinity of the boat and waited. Tuya tried to control her fears. It literally was impossible for her to escape the cavern any other way than to climb the rock wall. "At least we only have to make the attempt once," she said. "I can do anything once."

"You're a woman of courage." Khian smiled encouragement.

Glad to hear his admiring perception of her, Tuya tried to remind herself of the concept a few moments later when she stood at the base of the cliff, tied to Nikare by a makeshift rope of torn strips from the women's' dresses. Merneith was next in line, tied to her then the link went to Khian, who volunteered to bring up the rear. Tuya didn't have much confidence the rope would save her life if she fell, but it was better than nothing.

"Ready?" Nikare checked the expression of each one of his climbing partners. "My advice is to concentrate on the next handhold and foothold only. Don't look up, don't look down. Stay focused on the immediate next move. All right?"

Swallowing hard, Tuya rubbed her hands on her dress. "I'll do my best."

"I have no fear of heights that I know of," Merneith said. "Let's get this over with."

The ordeal began.

Tuya was never sure afterwards how long it took her to make the ascent, climbing awkwardly behind Nikare. He called down encouragement, and Khian checked on her from his post behind Merneith. Tuya shook with fear the entire time. About halfway up, Nikare had identified a ledge where he let the two women rest as he and Khian remained in their respective spots on the rock face, so as not to put too much weight on the stone where Tuya and Merneith clung, barely wide enough for their feet to rest. Then the Medjai started climbing again, and Tuya had no choice but to follow his lead.

Finally, blessedly, Nikare reached down to grasp her under the arms and lift her from the cave to the sands of the open desert, where she lay in the narrow sliver of shade. Merneith was assisted from the cave too, and Khian emerged last.

He untied the rope from himself and the musician and came to Tuya, kneeling beside her. "How are you doing? You were amazing on the climb, so determined."

"I feel as if I'm going to faint." She put a hand to her head. "I'm so thirsty."

"I can remedy that situation at least." He picked her up and carried her across the hot sands.

"Surely you're not planning to march in the middle of the day?" she asked in horror.

Laughing, he shook his head. "I can understand you've not taken in our improved situation. Nikare brought us to our own oasis." He swung her in his arms so she could see for herself the tiny stand of vegetation around a small pool of water.

"Blessed be the gods," she said in relief.

Khian set her down next to one of the palm trees then brought her water in his cupped hands. She drank greedily and felt partially revived, sitting up and staring at her surroundings. "Do we have any idea where we are?"

"I remember the map," Nikare said from his position sitting next to Merneith. "I believe this is a dot slightly to the north of the caravan route. We should be able to hike to the road tonight after the sun sets, and tomorrow we can implore an east bound group to give us assistance in reaching the garrison at the main oasis.

Unfortunately, my writ of authority from Pharaoh got soaked in all the activity with the boat, but we may find an official who knows me."

Khian opened the leather pouch at his belt and unrolled the tiny scroll. "Mine is in somewhat better state fortunately. At least the seal is intact."

Suddenly, a crescendo of jackal howls erupted, loud and eerie, coming from all sides. Khian rose, making sure the women were behind him.

"Ranefer?" Nikare asked, coming to stand beside him, knife drawn.

"I hope so." Khian shaded his eyes with one hand and stared toward the spot where they'd emerged from the caverns. He thought he saw movement and, a moment later, he was sure as a tall figure crawled onto the sands and rose to its feet in a fluid motion.

With a glad heart, Khian hurried forward to greet their companion. "Thank the Great Ones you survived. We'd never have made it past the cursed grate in the river if you'd not been there to destroy it."

Pausing well short of the oasis, Ranefer gave him a bow. "I was honored to help in your gods-given quest. The rest is up to you now, my brother." He extended his arms, appearing more fur covered and less human than Khian remembered. Still, without hesitation, Khian grasped the other's hands and they embraced as warriors do.

"I can never repay you sufficiently," Khian said.

"I don't know if the Lord of the Sacred Land will step in to assist you in the future, but I'd be honored to go into battle at your side again. You're a worthy packmate." Ranefer's voice was low, more like growling than words. "I pray you never need such help. Life, prosperity, and health to you and your mate."

Khian stepped aside. "The same to you."

He blinked as a large, striped jackal now stood where Ranefer had been but a heartbeat of time before. Throwing its head back, the animal howled and was answered by a chorus of voices from beyond the dunes. Without a second glance at him, the beast trotted to the west at a ground-covering pace.

"May Anubis stand between you and harm," he said to the departing jackal before making the return hike to the small oasis to rejoin his human companions. He resolved to take time to examine the ancient murals in the oldest family tombs when he got home to the Jackal Nome and see what he could find about the legendary connection to Anubis. *I'll be making generous tithes to the temple as well.*

The rest of the day the quartet slept in the shade, although Khian and Nikare alternated standing watch. Tuya had nightmares from which he had to awaken her, and her dazed condition each time concerned him, but she seemed to draw strength and reassurance from his presence. He sat and held her for the last few hours of the day and she slept soundly.

He wondered how much persuasion she was going to need to agree to marry him and take the chance inherent in moving to the Jackal Nome. She'd shared portions of her difficult childhood with him in whispered snippets during the boat ride, and he put those details together with a few things Hemaka had shared the first night while they waited at the nursemaid's home. *When we return to the known comforts and routine of the palace in a few days, will she lose her resolve?*

Which Great One should he pray to for help in making her love for him strong enough to overcome her fears of change? He knew he could safeguard her for the rest of their lives. Khian glanced at the sky and sent a silent plea to Mut for help in this private quest. No white winged vultures flew to acknowledge his request but, remembering the goddess's words to him in his vision, he felt hopeful.

As soon Ra's sun boat disappeared into the west, Khian led them to the east, and by dawn they were indeed standing beside the caravan road.

"When we do find a caravan to take us on," Khian said, "I want you all to swear on your ka we won't discuss our true adventure. I intend to say we were on a mission for Pharaoh and that's all anyone needs to know. Until we can explain Isidu-Ur to the Great One, it's no one else's business."

"Bedraggled as we are, we may have trouble getting a caravan master to stop long enough to listen to our shortened tale, much less to give aid. We resemble ruffians," Nikare said. "We'd better start hiking to the next oasis."

Khian knew, brave as his lady's heart was, she'd not much more to give in terms of strength.

It seemed Nikare shared his anxious doubts, for the Medjai said, "Or you three can wait here and see if a camel train comes along, while I make for the garrison at the oasis with all possible speed, to bring help."

"I hear bells," Tuya said from her spot beside the track.

Khian heard them as well. He drew his sword and planted himself in the center of the road.

The camel drover leading the oncoming caravan cursed and shook his fist, demanding Khian move aside, but he stood resolute. "In the name of Pharaoh, I, Captain Khian of the royal army, command your aid," he shouted, holding the stamped papyrus in his free hand. "Where is your caravan master, that I may make my needs known without delay?"

A man rode up on a well-appointed racing camel. "What's all this? Why have we stopped?"

"Are you the master?" Khian's temper was growing short.

"Aye, Ptahnetamun, who's asking and why?"

"I'm Captain Khian, charged with safeguarding the Lady Tuya, senior lady-in-waiting to the Royal Wife. We're in need of assistance to get to the next oasis and the garrison there."

The caravan master gave a huge guffaw. "You're in need of assistance all right, captain. You look more like a thief than an officer."

Tuya walked forward to join Khian, her movements as regal and graceful as if she'd been in the palace, attending the queen. "I recognize your name," she said to Ptahnetamun as camels and donkey carts detoured around them, raising clouds of dust. "My dear friend Lady Nima speaks of you fondly from time to time. Her husband the general less so. I'll be grateful for your aid for myself and my companions because, despite the best efforts of my guards, we've not eaten in nearly two days, and I cannot walk further. Pharaoh will be most generous in repayment for your help. Captain, show him the scroll of authority."

Ptahnetamun stared at her, eyes narrowed, then ordered his camel to kneel so he could dismount. He examined Khian's papyrus closely then bowed to Tuya. "I beg pardon, my lady, for not immediately coming to your assistance."

She accepted his apology with a graceful inclination of her head. "I understand we hardly present an honorable appearance as we stand here in our dust and rags. No doubt our story seems like a badly written scribe's tale."

The caravan master grabbed a passing drover from his tasks and barked orders. Soon a donkey cart came up the line, the animal trotting alertly under its driver's handling of the reins. The conveyance halted beside Ptahnetamun as several servants came running with waterskins and a basket which Khian devoutly hoped held food suitable for eating while on the trail.

"The cart is for you, my lady, and your companions," the caravan master said. "The water and food as well. I regret we can't stop to cook anything more sustaining."

"Whatever you have will be more than I've eaten this day or yesterday," she said graciously. "And will no doubt taste as good as the finest delicacies from Pharaoh's kitchen to me today."

Khian handed her into the cart, where she sat straight backed as Nikare helped Merneith join her. The two men walked alongside the cart. Tuya shared out the bread and fruit, which the group munched as the caravan proceeded eastward.

When the caravan arrived at the oasis in the early evening, Ptahnetamun sought out Khian, drawing him aside. "I'm having my men set up a spare tent for Lady Tuya and her companion. The commander'll not have adequate accommodations for her in the fort, and I've pulled from my own supplies to make her comfortable. I had my girls open the cargo panniers destined for the marketplace in Thebes and pull a few new clothes and shoes for both of the ladies."

"I'm grateful."

The caravan master eyed him. "I've no idea what the four of you endured out there in the desert, and I'm not asking, but I think you should consider traveling to Thebes with me. I tell you plainly, your lady seems at the end of her strength and, while you could reach the capital more rapidly in a chariot, I don't think it would be wise, not for her. Let her travel in comfort before she reports to Pharaoh."

"I agree," Khian said, in gratitude. "I'm sworn not to leave her side so all four of us would be your guests."

Ptahnetamun laughed in satisfied good humor. "Pharaoh's treasury can afford it. I've got enough highly taxed wine and spices on this trip, more deben for the Great One's coffers. He can pay me a little back. I'll be submitting my bill to the palace in due time for being such a gracious host."

Despite the master's mercenary words, Khian had the sense he was genuinely concerned about Tuya as well. Of course, he could have insisted on Ptahnetamun accommodating them further, but it was a relief to have the offer made of free will and good intent.

Tuya made no protest, only telling him she was happy with whatever he felt was the best course. Khian ushered her into the tent provided for her to share with Merneith and eyed the dinner set out for her with approval. "I must go talk to the commander at the fort," he said. "I want to send a message to the palace via homing pigeon, let them know you're alive and we're on our way to Thebes. It'll take a few days, especially as the message will have to go first to the military command where the bird is based and be relayed to the Great One, but at least word will arrive before we do."

She held his arm as he turned to leave. "You'll be back, though? You won't stay at the fort?"

He took her in his arms and kissed her tenderly. "Nikare will be right outside the tent in my absence, and I'll come to you as soon as I've finished my business at the fort, my word on it. What's amiss?"

"My experiences at these oases were as Meketre's captive, in chains, waiting to learn my fate. I'm not easy being here. I know you must think me foolish."

"Not at all," he said. "You've been though terrible experiences, things no one would believe if reading a scribe's tale, yet you endured them. It would be amazing indeed if you walked away unscathed. Even warriors suffer the pain of remembrance at times, visions of dire battles, of friends killed as they fought beside you." He stopped, biting his lip, reluctant to expose too much of his own struggle with the horrors of war. Gold of valor couldn't erase the experience of close combat.

"Truly? You're not just saying these things to make me feel better?"

"Perhaps men who've trained their entire lives to lead troops into battle are more inured to the carnage than someone like me, raised to be a farmer. I did what I had to do, for Pharaoh and for my men, but I hope never to have to go to war again. I've no regrets, and I did what was proper, under the laws of ma'at, to preserve the Black Lands."

"Your heart will be judged as worthy," she said with such certainty he thought maybe the goddess had spoken through her.

"I pray it be so. But now let me go and do my duty, that I may return to you while there's any dinner left." He made his tone light and teasing. "I know you and Merneith are prodigious eaters."

Laughing, Tuya waved a hand at the crowded table of bowls and platters the caravan's servants had brought. "I think we can spare you a few crumbs, my faithful warrior."

"You don't mind sharing the tent with her, do you? We might not have been successful in your rescue without her help—we owe her a great debt."

"Of course I don't mind. She's a sweet girl and I'm looking forward to helping her find her way at court." Tuya gave him a little push. "If you'd leave, I might be able to take a bath and try the pretty new clothes Ptahnetamun sent."

"I can take a hint." Happy to see her mood improved, he left the tent, sending Merneith in to join Tuya and exchanging a few quiet words with Nikare before he set off to the fort.

When he arrived at the tent later, business having taken much longer than he'd hoped, darkness had fallen. He found Merneith sitting beside the large pillows serving as Tuya's bed, keeping watch over the lady as she slept. Finger to her lips, she rose and drew Khian outside.

"She sleeps fitfully, bad dreams make her cry out," the musician said. "But she ate well enough."

"Thank you for taking care of her."

"The lady is a delightful companion. If everyone at court is like her—warm and welcoming—I'll be happy." She glanced at the Medjai, standing silently to the side. "Nikare promised to take me to the center of the oasis, where the dancers and musicians perform for extra deben. I'm so eager to hear current music and learn new tunes."

"We'll be there quite a long time, I've no doubt," Nikare said.

"Have fun then." Khian re-entered the tent. He pondered having a guard detail sent over from the fort, as it bothered him not to have someone standing watch. Ptahnetamun swore by his crew and the tight security they maintained. Indeed, Khian had seen a man plainly detailed to keep an eye on Tuya's tent. Deciding the precautions were enough for now, he wandered to the table and made a meal from the generous leftovers, washed down with an excellent wine Ptahnetamun had sent over earlier.

He sank into the cushions next to the bed and studied Tuya's face in the light from the oil lamps. She was beautiful, younger without the elaborate makeup a lady of the court wore.

As if feeling the weight of his gaze, she took a deep breath and opened her eyes, smiling as she saw him. "I'm glad you're here."

"No bad dreams?"

Frowning, she rubbed her forehead. "None I remember, at any rate. Where are Nikare and Merneith?"

"He invited her to spend the evening at the oasis, watching the entertainers. She's hungry for new music. Well, for new experiences of any kind, I gather."

"And you've eaten?"

He nodded. "And sampled this excellent wine."

"Good." Extending her hand gracefully, she took the wine from him and had several sips, glancing at him over the lip of the mug. "I find I'm quite restored to myself after eating dinner and a good nap."

He had his doubts, seeing the shadows under her eyes, but he was willing to agree if it pleased her.

Tuya set the wine down and took his hand, drawing him from the chair and onto the bed with her, shifting to make room for him. She wound her arms around his neck and pulled him close for a kiss, her tongue tracing the seam of his lips delicately. Pulling her soft body against him, Khian caressed her tongue with his own, tasting the wine and a bit of honey flavor from dinner. She felt so good in his arms, his body responded to her nearness, his manhood hardening in a mere moment and pressing against the soft vee of her thighs. Tuya murmured his name as he thrust against her, both of them frustrated by the layers of their clothing.

He broke off the kiss, softening the move by trailing tiny caresses down her neck. He stroked her breast, finding the nipple pebbled and ready for his attention. She tugged at his tunic, trying to remove it. Khian caught her hands and gazed into her eyes. "Are you sure you've recuperated enough?"

Tuya laughed and guided his hand under her skirt, to part the soft hairs and touch the delicate skin of her most private places. He found her slick and ready for him, and his cock jumped at the thought of plunging deep into her. "You caught my eye at the gold of valor ceremony," she said, reclining on the plumped pillows as he worked his fingers into the cleft. He delighted in the way her breath came faster, making it a challenge for her to continue speaking coherent thoughts. Biting her lip, Tuya squirmed under him in delicious pleasure as he teased the tiny bud of sensitive flesh at her entrance. "I think I've been ready to experience what you offer since that moment, my valiant warrior." She gasped as he penetrated deeper, moving his fingers in a sensuous massage to bring her to the moment of ecstasy.

"Even when you were angry I'd tagged along where you didn't want me to be?" he teased, watching her expressive face and relishing her enjoyment of his attentions.

Tuya took a deep breath, moaning with pleasure and tumbled into orgasm before collapsing onto the pillows with a well satisfied smile. "In light of your talents, I forgive you for past annoyances. But not if you leave all these clothes on." Tugging at the tunic again, she said, "Lovely as you made me feel just now, I want the benefit of that stout cock I feel pressing against me, which I vow can provide me a thousand pleasures, but not unless you free it from its current entrapment. Bring to the light that which is hidden."

"Who can refuse a lady of the court? Especially when our minds are one in this desire?" He stood and pulled his tunic over his head, then unbuckled the belt holding his kilt in place and allowed the garment to fall to the floor, leaving him in loincloth only, the bulge where his impatient cock and aching balls waited for freedom prominent. Keeping his eyes on Tuya, whose unabashedly admiring looks aroused him further, Khian unwound the last fabric between him and his desires. His arousal jutted proudly when it was freed, and her gasp fed his flames.

She sat up to remove her dress, and he helped her, his hands clumsy with the desire and passion consuming him. Her breasts were full and high, perfect to his eyes and, as she lay against the pillows, he came over her, spending a few precious moments tasting and sampling the pebbled nipples and satin flesh, allowing his tongue to tease more arousal from her.

Impatient, Tuya reached for his cock, lying pressed against her most sensitive flesh and guided him inside, moving her hips to draw him further into the incredible warmth of her body. The sensations overwhelmed him, and he drove deep, barely regaining his control enough to pause and kiss her. "I've longed for this," he whispered. "You're so beautiful—everything I've ever dreamed of embodied in one person. When I feared I'd lost you—"

"Sssh." She laid her hand on his lips, and he kissed them as she said, "I know, my love. I felt the same when I feared I'd never see you again, never have the chance to tell you what was in my heart. But here we are now thanks to the gods and Pharaoh and your bravery. I ask for nothing more than to see your face every day of my life."

"Don't deny your own courage," he said, refusing to let her count her own contribution as less. "You survived and grew stronger."

She locked her legs at his waist, behind his back, pulling him deeper and putting unbearably pleasurable pressure on his cock. Losing all focus on whatever words he'd planned to utter, Khian gave himself to the climax building within him. He thrust hard, and Tuya met him move for move until they were so closely joined he was sure they'd become one person. He spilled his seed in a final moment of ecstasy, wrapped around the woman he loved.

She threw her head back, moaning his name as she arched under him in her own release. They collapsed together, warm and satiated.

"I've never been so happy." He stroked her tousled hair off her face, losing himself in her luminous brown eyes. "You will be my wife, won't you? I love you more than I can express, not even if we have another million years together. I'll never stop trying to tell you how I feel, this I swear."

Delicious little sensual tremors still ran through her body, where Khian remained seated, both of them readying their energies for more passion, she was sure. Khian's blunt words were more meaningful to her ears than all the elegant poems the queen's poets could recite, or even the poetry he himself had spoken to her because he truly meant them. The sentiments were just for her. "Yes, of course I'll marry you. We're halves of a single heart when it comes to love." She stroked her hand along his broad, muscular back before cupping his rear and squeezing. Unable to stop smiling, she added, "As you promised me on the boat, you've been very persuasive."

He raised himself up on one elbow to give her a serious look. "Are you sure? Can you bring yourself to leave your life in Thebes to be with me?"

"How can I stay in Thebes without you?" she said simply. "My heart would break." She drew him closer for a kiss, and there was no more conversation.

Khian fell asleep in her arms after they'd finished making love for the second time and bathed themselves as best they could with the basin of water and cloths Tuya'd been given by the caravan master's servants.

Tuya herself was wide awake, having napped off and on in the donkey cart, propped against Merneith's shoulder, and a deeper sleep in the tent while he went to the fort to conduct business. She rubbed his back and, when he rolled over in his sleep, she curled up to him, his strong body like a warm wall behind her, protective and reassuring.

Pillowing her head on her arm, she pondered her return to Thebes. She was glad they were going to stay with the caravan rather than make a mad dash in open chariots. There was nothing pressing to tell Pharaoh, since Isidu-Ur was hardly situated to wage war on Egypt, and she relished the idea of more time to spend with Khian out of the too curious eyes of the many gossips at court. She'd been a lady-in-waiting far too long not to know how people would talk about her going to the provincial Jackal Nome to marry a man who wasn't even of noble birth. Although his gold of valor and amkhu honors from Pharaoh's hand carried status and weight. The fact he was a landowner wouldn't hurt either.

Idly, she asked herself if she really cared about the snide remarks she'd undoubtedly receive, the assumption she'd settled for Khian after rejecting suitors of far more elevated birth and means in previous years. *No one knows the truth of my heart but me, and all I want is Khian now and in the afterlife.* Ashayet would be happy for her and was, Tuya realized a bit painfully, her only true friend in Thebes. She moved among the courtiers and the nobility of the city, but always a step or two apart. Smiles, clever comments, and false faces were her daily routine.

Why had she allowed herself to be so trapped in the palace life? Was it truly just the comfort? The prestige of her post in Ashayet's inner circle?

Her fear of change was powerful, she had to admit to herself.

I never found the right man, the right partner, to make me feel safe in stepping away from the surety of court. Someone whose heart I could weigh in the balance of the goddess Ma'at 's scales and find equal to mine.

Khian murmured her name and curled even more tightly around her.

Finally ready to drift off to sleep herself, now eager to begin the adventure in a completely different life, Tuya closed her eyes. "Children," she said to herself with a smile. Perhaps the gods had blessed them with the beginnings of a new life already this night. Khian was certainly a strong and inexhaustible lover. Seeing a vision of sons with his features and daughters with hers, she allowed her eyelids to close and sleep to take her.

Chapter Eleven

A few days later, she stood in the bustling caravan center on the edge of Thebes, trying hard to hold onto her calm, as memories of the last time she'd been there rose in her mind. Khian had gone to find a litter for her. Nikare and Merneith stood close by.

Ptahnetamun had said his farewells, accepted her thanks with grace and laughed heartily about the magnificent bill he was going to send to the Chief Scribe. He and his crew were now busy unloading their camels and dealing with departing passengers and new arrivals. It felt odd to Tuya to have been such a part of the caravan for a few days and now separate from it. She supposed this was how being back in the palace was going to seem as well. Maybe she didn't fit anywhere any more. Smiling at the idea, because it further encouraged her to make the move to the Jackal Nome, she saw Khian returning with a conveyance for her.

They made good time through Thebes, although not as efficiently as a litter from the palace would have done, with its attendant guards. Neither Khian nor Tuya had wanted to linger in the caravan hub long enough to send word to the palace and wait for someone to dispatch the entourage she was due.

"Much more efficient to get ourselves to the palace," Khian said.

The palace guards were dubious, since even in her borrowed clothing Tuya in no way resembled a high ranking lady of the court, but Khian flashed his papyrus with Pharaoh's seal again. An officer was sent for, who luckily knew Tuya and she was escorted with much deference to one of the smaller audience rooms in Pharaoh's wing of the palace.

"The Great One will be with you as soon as he's done with his audience with the Minoan ambassador," the officer said before saluting and leaving the room.

Tuya flung herself into a chair and laughed. "So far, not an overwhelming reaction to my homecoming."

"In fairness, we did try to keep the whole matter quiet," Khian said. "Since, at the time Nikare and I left Thebes, no one had any idea of the truth of what had happened or where you were. Until we know Pharaoh's wishes in the matter it's best to be discreet."

The door flew open and the Royal Wife rushed in, leaving her fan bearers and guards hurrying to keep up. "Tuya! I hardly dared to hope we'd meet again in this life."

The two women embraced, while the others made proper obeisance to the queen.

Ashayet had tears in her eyes. "I prayed nightly to the goddess Mut to help you—I can't wait to hear the tale. You're so thin and pale—are you all right?"

"I'm fine, Great One, thank you for your concern and your prayers." Tuya beamed as she looked at Khian, standing at attention. "I had two wonderful rescuers. And please allow me to introduce Merneith, a citizen of—of the place I was held captive. She was a tremendous help to us in our escape—she's a harpist. Can we find room for her in your inner court?"

Merneith had gone to 'kiss the earth', head lowered respectfully. Ashayet walked to her, raising the woman to her feet and hugging her. "Anyone who assisted in bringing my beloved friend Tuya safely home to me shall be richly rewarded. Of course I have need for another talented musician—what court ever has enough people who can create beautiful songs?" With the warm comment, the queen stripped one of her own bracelets off and clasped the golden circlet around Merneith's arm. "A small token of my gratitude."

While Merneith stammered her thanks, Ashayet returned to Tuya and drew her aside.

The private door at the rear of the room opened, and Pharaoh himself strode in, smiling. "I'm most pleased to see you back among us, Lady Tuya," he said as the men saluted and the women genuflected. "And I await your account of how this was accomplished, captain."

"We believed we should report at once, Great One, and not tarry to make ourselves more presentable." Khian was calm. "This tale may require some time to unwind for you, sir."

"And the fewer ears the better, eh?" Pharaoh gestured to the captain of the guard. "Clear the room, send for my Chief Scribe and have food and drink brought. Meetings with ambassadors such as the ones I endured before this hour can be dry work, and I'm thirsty."

There was a flurry of activity as his orders were obeyed and the room cleared. Edekh joined them while the others filed out. Nat-re-Akhte seated himself on the gilded chair. Ashayet brought him wine and a plate of dates and other tempting fruits, before seating herself in the smaller chair next to his. Edekh stood behind them.

"Great Ones, if I could make a request on behalf of the Lady Tuya before we begin," Khian said, "She's been through quite an ordeal, and I believe it might be best if she were allowed to sit."

Tuya immediately made protesting noises, but Pharaoh nodded his agreement while Ashayet glanced sharply between the captain and her lady-in-waiting, a knowing smile hovering on her lips.

Although Tuya had to speak first, to explain how the note came to her and what transpired when she went to the caravan hub, Khian bore the brunt of reciting their adventures, giving his report of events. Nikare chimed in on certain facts falling within his purview as a police officer. Listening to him discuss the death of her half-brother made Tuya nauseous, but she believed justice had been served, after what Anen had done to her.

Pharaoh frowned at certain details and had quick, incisive questions. Edekh asked a question or two himself, principally about the lost city of Isidu-Ur. Merneith, trembling and frightened, was called upon to answer many of the questions, about the size of the city and how many people remained there.

Graciously, Pharaoh interrupted one of her answers to give reassurance. "I know my queen has already welcomed you to our home. I wish to add my thanks for your part in assisting my officers to rescue Lady Tuya from peril. A royal allowance shall be settled upon you and living space in the palace granted. No harm shall come to you while you're under my protection."

"Th—thank you, Great One. I had no idea how big and overwhelming the world outside the city truly was."

Leaning back in his chair, Pharaoh made a small hand sign as if to dismiss the topic. "Now to revisit the issue of how many rabisu the authorities in the lost city have to call upon—"

When the tale was told, with all its miraculous aspects, Pharaoh sat silently for a moment. "So it seems the Isidu-Ur are much depleted after your visit, Captain Khian. Well done. I feel there's no immediate threat from their direction, although we'd best keep an extra eye on caravans passing through the area. Order more patrols." He directed the command at Edekh who made further notes. "And, as the Great Ones themselves assisted you personally, including with the matter of the immortal queen, I'm satisfied the threat has been eradicated. It is my command no one shall speak of this lost city outside this room. Let the Halaqu dwindle and die off on their own, let no enemy of Egypt think to enlist them as allies. Officer Nikare, your Medjai will also have to keep watch, to make sure the criminal activities don't recommence at the hands of those bearing the butterfly and scorpion tattoos."

"We'll be on guard, sir."

"Make no mistake, I *will* take my army, go in and find a way to wipe Isidu-Ur out if the situation changes, but for now I've got other, more pressing uses for my generals and their troops. It bothers me to leave the descendants of the Egyptian prisoners in the city, as captives, however, even if they now believe themselves to be citizens of the place. The matter, with all its complications, requires more thought and consultation with the gods as to their will, but is not your concern." He addressed Edekh. "An additional lump sum from the royal treasury, to Captain Khian and Officer Nikare, for services rendered to Pharaoh."

The Chief Scribe acknowledged the order. Tuya wondered if he was going to dock the awarded sum for the loss of a war chariot and team, but this was certainly the wrong moment to raise the issue, even in jest.

"Caravan master Ptahnetamun to receive my thanks for his care of Lady Tuya, his bill to be paid when presented and a ten percent reward added for services rendered." It seemed Pharaoh was done with his commands. "Captain Khian, you are released from my personal service to rejoin your company and its assignments in Thebes. Officer Nikare, you are to wait upon me in two days' time, to discuss a new matter that has arisen, having nothing to do with this concluded episode." He rose and held out a hand to his wife. "Truly, an amazing afternoon of marvels and adventure. No scribe's tale can compare. "

Tuya and the others bowed low as he and the Royal Wife left the room through the private door.

Edekh lingered. "I'll send scribes to find you if anything else arises. Lady Merneith, if you'll come with me, I'll have you escorted to your new chambers. Lady Tuya, we're truly blessed to have among our company again. You'll find everything in order in your rooms. Tonight we have no scheduled events, but tomorrow there's the banquet for the ambassadors and, of course, the queen will expect you to attend."

How fast the old life closes in to entangle me. Tuya's heart sank. There'd been no opportunity to mention her desire to wed Khian and leave Thebes. A person of her station couldn't just abandon her duties – consent was required from the queen and from Pharaoh, who would most likely accede to his wife's wishes in the matter, but he still had to be properly petitioned. Tuya resolved to speak to Ashayet at the first auspicious moment, probably in a few days. She knew there was also a ceremony at the temple later in the week as well, where she'd have to sing and play her part.

Edekh took Merneith away. Nikare shook hands with Khian and hugged Tuya then he too was gone.

"You look vexed," she said to Khian now the room was empty.

"As do you." He came to her and smoothed the frown from her brow.

"It wasn't the right time to ask him for permission to marry," she said.

"I bow to your knowledge of Pharaoh and court protocol."

Responding to the stiffness in his tone, she hastened to explain. "I'm not having second thoughts—once the Great One was delivering his judgments and orders, the time was gone for requests."

Khian hugged her. "I believe you. Does something else trouble you?"

Tuya reached for his hand. "I feel the coils of court life sneaking around me from all sides again."

"Don't let them," he said urgently, giving her a kiss. "Shall I lend you my sword to slash yourself free?"

She smiled at the idea, but his next words had her frowning again.

"May I escort you to your rooms before I go?" He offered her his arm and a bow.

Her heart was pounding, and she could scarcely believe what he'd said. "Go where? Aren't you staying with me? I'm allowed to entertain anyone I choose in my own apartment, there'd be no problem."

"I'm still an officer under orders in the army," he said. "Pharaoh told me to report to my company, and I must go present myself to my commander. There was no dispensation, no encouragement to wait until tomorrow because a delay would please me."

"Only because he doesn't know we're in love," she said. "Pharaoh is a kind man – he wouldn't mind if we took one more night together."

"I'm not a Great One who can order the universe to suit my convenience." Khian shook his head. "We'll straighten matters out soon enough but, for now, I must go. You don't want to visit me in the military prison because I'm accused of being derelict in my duties. I'm sure it's a grim place, even worse perhaps than Isidu-Ur."

She understood he was trying to tease, to cheer her up, but Tuya's mood grew more somber the closer she came to her rooms and the moment of parting. Hemaka stood beside the door and clapped his hands in joy as he caught sight of her. The elderly servant embraced her quickly, because there were other people in the corridor, staring at the emotional scene. Tuya was forced to say her goodbyes to Khian in formal words, with only a snatched kiss as comfort. She walked into her bedroom, took one look at the bed, and burst into tears.

"There, there, of course you're overwrought. I'm sure you must have been through a terrible ordeal, as thin and tired as you've become." Hemaka patted her shoulder. "But you're home and soon enough your life will be in its proper state of balance, as if you'd never left."

She cried all the harder, for a long time, until she felt unable to breathe properly. Then she allowed Hemaka to bring her a basin of cool water to wash her face and told him a brief, highly edited version of events.

"I'm sure the best thing is to take a long bath, don your own clean nightgown, and sleep soundly," the elderly servant said. "I'll send in your maids."

She caught his hand. "Thank you for going to Khian as soon as you found the cursed note. You saved my life."

"Then I'm grateful to the gods and to the captain. Will we be seeing him again, my lady?"

"Oh yes."

Hemaka winked and left the room to summon the maids. Alone for the first time in a long time, Tuya wandered out to her tiny garden and sat, staring at the fountain and fish pond. "I refuse to sink back into court life," she said, putting all the defiance she could muster into her voice, not sure who she was defying. Fate maybe?

Despite Pharaoh's words of praise and the monetary reward, Khian left the palace a discontented man. Edekh caught him on the stairs right before he'd have reached the exit.

"I've been looking for you. Pharaoh ordered a chariot to take you to the barracks," the Chief Scribe said.

Khian nodded, his belief confirmed that he was indeed expected to report promptly to his commanding officer. "Too kind of the Great One. I regret deeply I had to leave the one assigned to me in the desert, as well as the horses."

As they walked toward the courtyard where the chariot would be waiting, Edekh laughed. "I chalk the loss up to Nikare's running tally with me and will give him endless grief over it. But, in truth, you heard Pharaoh yourself, agreeing you took the only action proper at the time. No blame attaches to either of you. Rescuing Tuya and solving a problem we didn't even know we had, as far as the existence of the lost city, has earned you the Great One's true gratitude. Besides, the animals carry Pharaoh's cartouche so we may yet reacquire them from a nomad tribe desirous of a reward."

"It was a pleasure to meet you," Khian said, offering his hand to Edekh.

"Likewise. I'm only sorry you won't be staying with us in Thebes for a longer time."

"When my enlistment is done, I must get my men and myself home to the Jackal Nome and get the seeds in before planting season passes." Khian shook his head. "Farming is my true vocation."

"Egypt needs her farmers just as much as she needs her soldiers." Edekh clapped him on the shoulder and turned to re-enter the palace.

Khian was driven to the barracks by an efficient member of Pharaoh's Own Guard who, if puzzled why he was detailed to provide transportation to a mere provincial captain, asked no questions and was polite.

There seemed to be a lot of activity at the complex, and Khian strode inside to find his commander then his own second in command. Luckily the man appeared in the corridor and his demeanor changed as if merely seeing Khian had lifted some huge burden from his shoulders. "Thank the gods you're back."

"What's amiss?"

"We've received orders to sail for home tomorrow morning. I've been running around all day getting the men organized, and what must cursed donkey's son Itu do last night before the orders came down but get thrown into Thebes' jail for causing a fight at a tavern? With members of Pharaoh's palace guard, mind you. I think the men were gambling with the wagers running too high. There were allegations of cheating on both sides and too much beer. Maybe even a woman or two involved. Three more of our men are locked up with Itu—we can't sail for home tomorrow and leave them to rot. Now you can go with me to plead for their release. I was afraid the authorities wouldn't listen to me alone, but you have gold of valor and Pharaoh's ear."

"Trust me, the Great One doesn't want to hear from me about drunken soldiers. I'll be with you in a few moments, but first I must report in." Khian's heart was heavy, and his head ached. There'd be no time to make a quick trip to the palace and see Tuya, much less to explain about his leaving Thebes in the morning. He wished the caravan had been less efficient in conveying them to the capital. If he'd arrived after his men had left, he'd have been upset but would have had the necessary time to arrange matters regarding a marriage with Tuya.

"I'll be in the courtyard then," said his second in command. "We should get to the jail well before sunset."

"I understand." Khian made haste to the commander's office. It was as if Shai, the god of Fate, was playing with them yet again. What had Mut said, that once she'd asked for a favor for Tuya, Fate allowed others to interfere with her life? Resulting in a huge mess they'd only just escaped from by the skin of their teeth.

As he waited to be announced to the general, he realized once he got to the Jackal Nome, he'd be forced to remain there for months to supervise the all-important planting. Tuya was nowhere near over her nightmares and already felt the pull of her court life—how well would she hold up in his enforced absence?

Tuya woke in the morning with her decision firmly in her mind and heart. Stretching, she contemplated the richly appointed bedroom and knew she'd miss the comforts here in the palace, but nothing was worth losing Khian and his love. She couldn't wait to see him and plan their approach to Pharaoh, possibly in a week or so. He'd grant them a private audience, she was sure. Maybe the queen would even give a small banquet in their honor after the marriage ceremony had taken place.

Making plans, she was leisurely with her bath, lingering to savor the remaining days in luxury. She'd get permission from the chief scribe to show Khian the royal zoo today and, while in the privacy of the gardens, they could speak together of their love and of the future.

She'd just gotten out of the water, swathed herself in a robe and begun her makeup when there was a knock at her door. Hoping it was Khian arriving early, she danced to the portal and drew the screen aside only to find Hemaka.

"Good morning, old friend. This is indeed an excellent day," she said, resuming her contemplation of the silver mirror, holding first one pair of earrings then another to her face to gauge the effect.

"A scroll was brought from the officers' barracks," he said, bowing.

Tuya wheeled. "Oh, I hope he doesn't have special duty today. I was counting on seeing him. We have something major to discuss."

"I hope all is well then."

She took the scroll and broke the seal, perusing the lines with a sinking heart.

Beloved,

My men and I have received our separation orders and sail for home today on the Dawn Racer. I asked for an extension but was denied.

With a cry, she dropped the scroll from suddenly nerveless fingers. Hemaka scooped it from the floor as she sank into her favorite chair.

"Bad news?"

"The worst—he's leaving. But how can he?" She sank down on the bed. "It's Fate—he's not done with me yet. I've been shown the answer to my future and now Shai wants to take it away again."

"Best read it all, my lady."

She took the papyrus back with trembling hands and read it out loud.

I'm truly sorry not to see you today, but perhaps it's for the best. I know I ask a great deal of you, to leave the court and give up everything you know to risk a life in the rural province with me as a mere landholder's wife. I shouldn't rush you. Take this time to reflect and, I swear on my honor as an officer, I'll return for you as soon as I can.

"As soon as he can," she said brokenly. "The implication is he'll travel here after the planting, after the harvesting—anything could happen in so much time. He's explained to me thoroughly what a long process it is at this season, and he must be there to supervise."

Apparently, Hemaka was absorbing the shock of his mistress's plan to leave Thebes and move to the Jackal Nome. Or perhaps he felt he had to remain calm since she was so obviously not. "Does he say anything else?"

"Only that he loves me and always will."

"There's your answer then," Hemaka said. "All things in time."

"No." She rose to her feet, wiping away tears. "No, I'm done with waiting and marking time. I have to go now, *right now*. If he'd waited to come after me when I was kidnapped, I'd have died." She ran to the baskets holding her dresses and grabbed the one on top, heedless of which it might be. Dumping out the basket next to it, she crammed two more dresses in the container, emptied her jewel box and, while Hemaka faced the door, she threw off her robe and put on the dress and sandals. She took a moment to don her wig. Grabbing a cloak, she rushed to the door, basket handle over her arm.

"What are you doing?" He followed her into the corridor.

"Going to see the queen."

"Like this? You're not properly dressed—" Hemaka scooped up an earring after the bauble tumbled from her basket, then a scarf, and ran after her again.

"I don't care." Fear gave her strength and resolve. As the senior lady-in-waiting she had unlimited access to the Royal Wife's apartments and, while the guards stared at her disheveled appearance, they stood aside for her.

Ashayet looked up in concern. "Tuya dear, whatever is wrong?"

"I wish to resign, with love and respect, Great One, but I must leave Thebes today."

"You just returned from your ordeal in the desert." The queen motioned for the two maids working on her wig and makeup to withdraw. "What's driven you to this decision?"

"Love, my lady. I'm in love with Captain Khian. He asked me to go with him—"

"Surely even a rural captain knows to give a lady time to withdraw from court properly, to assemble her possessions, settle matters?" Ashayet frowned. "This seems uncharacteristic of him."

Tuya thrust the note at her, breaking into tears. "I failed to ask Pharaoh for permission last night and now this morning Khian's been ordered from Thebes. It's the hand of Fate, tugging on the threads of my life yet again."

"I see." The queen read the note quickly then came to Tuya, hugging her. "Khian says he'll be back, dear. Calm yourself. He obviously loves you—his actions to find and rescue you prove his steadfastness beyond a shadow of a doubt. 'Tis but a delay."

"You don't understand," Tuya said, forgetting in her distress she was addressing the queen. "The goddess Mut told me I was nearly bricked into my life, nearly trapped into dying unloved, unwed, without children, because of my choices, of always retreating to my safe place at court, never taking risks. She said she was giving me one last chance. I must go with Khian now." She tapped her chest over the heart. "I know this with every fiber of my being. I'm terrified of losing this one opportunity to be with the man I love, of having a future together. Anything could happen if I don't seize this chance with my two fists and take the risk. The Great One Mut told Khian the god Shai played games with my life once already, and I refuse to give him a second chance." She knew she'd raised her voice and risked the wrath of a god, but she was too upset to control her emotions.

Chief Scribe Edekh came into the room and halted, mouth open in surprise at the scene in front of him. "I can consult with you later, Great One. I see you're quite occupied at the moment."

"When does the ship *Dawn Racer* leave?" Ashayet said.

He blinked. "I'm not aware of the specific vessel, my lady, but if the ship's master didn't sail at first tide, he'd be departing at the sixth hour. Quite soon."

"Not much time," the queen said to Tuya. "You'd never get to the docks before the ship leaves. The decision may already be out of your hands."

A new voice spoke, calm and slightly amused. "Clearly, there's a crisis brewing here."

With dismay, Tuya realized Pharaoh had entered the room.

The queen hugged her as she addressed her husband. "Our Tuya has fallen in love with Captain Khian to no one's surprise, and your army has shipped the man off today, inconveniently before the pair could marry. She was hoping to catch his ship and travel to his home with him, rather than wait until after the harvest, but Edekh says the boat may have already sailed or is soon to leave."

"Forgive me, Great Ones, for bothering you with my personal problems." Tuya curtseyed, although it was probably much too late for protocol. She thought she saw the chief scribe hiding a smile. "We wished to ask you for permission to wed yesterday, but there were much weightier matters at hand, and the time didn't seem auspicious."

A young scribe ran in, halting in mid-step and making deep obeisance when he realized Pharaoh was present.

"Who are you and what news do you bring us?" the ruler asked.

"I keep the records of the ships used in connection with military matters," he said in a threadbare voice. "How may I serve you, Great One?"

"I sent for him," Edekh explained. "At what hour does the *Dawn Racer* leave port?"

The junior scribe dropped one papyrus roll as he tried to unroll the other. Edekh steered him to as table and the young scribe ran his shaking finger down the list of vessels. "Mid-morning, my lord. Virtually any moment, in fact."

Pharaoh pointed at Edekh. "Send a runner to the port now, tell the harbor master to hold the ship." He came to Tuya. "You're sure? Khian is a good man, valorous, keeps the principles of ma'at, and owns a large estate, but it won't be anything like life here in Thebes."

"If I'm with the man I love, I don't care where we are. He and I endured much together, as you know, sir. Nothing is a hardship if he's by my side. Even in Isidu-Ur I knew all would be well when I saw him fight his way into the room to face the queen and her demons, to rescue me."

Nat-re-Akhte nodded. "All right then. Up to another adventure?"

"My lord?"

"Bring your basket and follow me." He dropped a kiss on Ashayet's cheek. "You'll owe me, my love, for arriving with a solution at hand."

"A debt I'll happily pay later. For now, get this girl to the ship." Ashayet gave Tuya a hug. "May the gods bless you. Send word of how you and Khian go on, and especially when there are to be children."

Tuya blushed. "You've always been so good to me, my dear friend. I'm sorry for leaving you so suddenly."

"I'll miss you terribly, but I'm relieved you're to have your happiness." Ashayet swiped a tear from her cheek.

"If you wish to reach the harbor in time, we need to depart now." Interrupting the leave taking, Pharaoh strode toward the door, and Tuya had to run to keep up.

"We'll send your household goods, once we have word all is settled," Edekh said.

Hemaka ran with her as she accompanied the ruler through the palace.

"Thank you for all your service," Tuya said to her elderly servant although she could barely talk as she rushed to keep up with Pharaoh. "Enjoy those grandchildren and sit in the sun every day."

"I'll miss you," he said and her heart clenched at the gleam of tears in his eyes.

They emerged in a large courtyard where three chariots stood waiting, one of which was Pharaoh's own, decorated with golden insignia, including his cartouche, and flying his flag. The ruler turned to Tuya. "Brave enough to ride in a war chariot?"

She answered with no hesitation or anxiety. "Anything to reach Khian."

"All right then." He marched to the chariots, shouting orders to his men.

Tuya kissed Hemaka then ran to the chariots. Her eyes went a little wide as Pharaoh hopped into his own then reached back a hand to her. She hadn't realized he meant to drive her *himself*. His spirited white horses stamped and tossed their heads, making the feathers on their elaborate bridles dance in the sunshine.

"We go to the harbor instead of on a training run," Nat-re-Akhte said to his men. "Full speed."

As Pharaoh took the reins and the team set off at a gallop, she clung to the rail of the chariot. The other two chariots drove slightly to the rear and flanking his. The herald in the second chariot blew the royal fanfare long and loud on his horn, alerting whoever might be ahead that Pharaoh was on the way and the road must be cleared.

The ruler drove with consummate skill, never slackening his pace, taking the curves without lifting a wheel from the road. Tuya had no fear, but was full of amazement at traveling like the wind, driven by the Great One himself.

The chariots swept into the harbor area, the herald blowing the clarion call over and over. *Pharaoh comes.*

A large ship sat beside the dock ahead. Men were busy unfastening the thick ropes holding the vessel to the dock and Tuya feared she was too late, even with the immense speed of Pharaoh's horses.

She heard shouts and a group of men ran onto the dock. "Hold that ship! Pharaoh's orders!"

All motion on the dock stopped as Nat-re-Akhte and the others drew their chariots to a halt a moment later. The ruler handed the reins to the soldier beside him and turned to Tuya with a good-natured laugh. "It seems we're in time."

"I'm so appreciative, Great One." As he personally handed her from the chariot, she said, "The journey was the most amazing few moments of my entire life. I'll have the tale painted on my tomb wall."

He leaned closer, patting her hand. "I've always wanted an excuse to gallop through the city since I was a boy first learning to drive a team. A secret between us."

Several men had approached cautiously and were now bowing.

"Good job holding the ship, Harbor Master," Pharaoh said. "I'm well pleased. Who is the captain of this vessel?"

"I am, my lord." A stout individual stood forth.

"I have another passenger for you, a lady of my court. Treat her with all due deference that she may send me a favorable report of her journey and your skills as a sailor."

"Of course, Great One. I'll assign her my own cabin."

Pharaoh nodded. "Summon Captain Khian from among the passengers on board."

One of his own men saluted and dashed to the gangplank, calling for Khian to attend the ruler.

Tuya thought her heart would burst with happiness as her beloved marched down the gangplank and across the wharf next to the senior officer. She ran to him and they embraced.

"You came," he said in a wondering tone. "I would have come to Thebes for you immediately after harvest, as I promised."

"I know," she said, "I had no doubts. But I couldn't bear to wait. The goddess told me long ago to seize the moment. I love you, and I want to be wherever you are, for the rest of my life."

Pharaoh cleared his throat. Embarrassed, Tuya faced the Great One, Khian at her side, standing at attention and saluting.

"It seems I didn't give you everything the gods felt you were due, upon our first official meeting scant weeks ago, captain," Nat-re-Akhte said to Khian with a broad smile. "Gold of valor, the right of amkhu *and* a loving wife plucked from my court. The queen and I'll miss Tuya, but she's spent many years in our service and now we wish her—and you—life, prosperity, and health. May you have much happiness, and a house full of children. Go with my blessing." He pivoted to return to his chariot, leaping into the vehicle with all the vigor of a much younger warrior.

His guards mounted their own vehicles, and the phalanx thundered away from the docks at a more restrained pace than they'd arrived.

Tuya heard the horn call one final time. Tears pricked her eyes, but she resolutely blinked them away.

"Regrets?" Khian took her in his arms and studied her face.

"Absolutely none."

"My lady, captain, if you'll follow me on board, we can still catch the tide," the ship's master said deferentially.

Grinning, Khian took her basket, which had been placed to the side by one of Pharaoh's soldiers. "You travel light yet again."

"The chief scribe promised to ship my other belongings," she said.

As they followed the captain up the gangplank, she heard one of the sailors exclaim as birds called overhead.

"Vultures don't frequent the harbor."

Shocked, Tuya glanced up in time to see a flock of the beautiful white birds, sacred to Mut, wheeling in the sky above the ship. A single white feather drifted down gracefully on the breeze off the Nile, and Khian leaned over the water as he reached out a hand to catch it. "A gift from your goddess perhaps?"

"Perhaps." She laughed and threw her arms around his neck. "I think you were my gift from the goddess actually."

"And you're mine, from the hand of Pharaoh himself."

"Were two people ever so blessed?" she asked, staring into his eyes.

"Never," he said.

***

Thank you for reading LADY OF THE NILE! I really hope you enjoyed the adventure (and of course I'd love a review if you have time and the inclination to write one – even a few sentences would be wonderful. Authors relish reader feedback).

•If you'd like to stay up to date on all my new releases, please sign up for my newsletter.

ABOUT VERONICA SCOTT

USA Today Best Selling Author

"SciFi Encounters" columnist for the USA Today Happy Ever After blog

Veronica Scott grew up in a house with a library as its heart. Dad loved science fiction, Mom loved ancient history and Veronica thought there needed to be more romance in everything. When she ran out of books to read, she started writing her own stories.

Seven time winner of the SFR Galaxy Award, as well as a National Excellence in Romance Fiction Award, Veronica is also the proud recipient of a NASA Exceptional Service Medal relating to her former day job, not her romances!

She was honored to read the part of Star Trek Crew Member in the audiobook production of Harlan Ellison's "The City On the Edge of Forever."

Blog: https://veronicascott.wordpress.com/
Twitter: https://twitter.com/vscotttheauthor
Facebook:
https://www.facebook.com/pages Veronica-Scott/177217415659637?ref=hl

ALSO BY VERONICA SCOTT

Magic of the Nile
Ghost of the Nile
Healer of the Nile

Fantasy Romance:
The Captive Shifter